RED SAILS TO CAPRI

Fourteen-year-old Michele Pagano lives in a little village on the island of Capri. On the day that three strangers arrive and stay at his parents' inn, an incredible adventure and mystery begin.

"In this colorful story of Capri and the rediscovery of the Blue Grotto, the author is successful in capturing the charm of a mountainside village and the personality of an earnest young boy...the skillfully drawn climax completes a vivid and charming tale whose humor, wisdom and excitement make it something to be shared with delight."

—*Horn Book*

RED SAILS
TO CAPRI

BY ANN WEIL

DRAWINGS BY C. B. FALLS

Troll Associates

PUFFIN BOOKS
Published by the Penguin Group
Viking Penguin Inc., 40 West 23rd Street, New York, New York 10010, U.S.A.
Penguin Books Ltd, 27 Wrights Lane, London W8 5TZ, England
Penguin Books Australia Ltd, Ringwood, Victoria, Australia
Penguin Books Canada Ltd, 2801 John Street, Markham, Ontario, Canada L3R 1B4
Penguin Books (N.Z.) Ltd, 182-190 Wairau Road, Auckland 10, New Zealand

Penguin Books Ltd, Registered Offices: Harmondsworth, Middlesex, England

First published in the United States of America by Viking Penguin Inc., 1952
Published in Puffin Books 1988
7 9 10 8 6
Copyright Ann Weil, 1952
Copyright renewed Jon Weil and Robert Weil, 1980
All rights reserved
Library of Congress catalog number: 88–42966
ISBN 0–14–032858–0

Printed in the United States of America
by R.R. Donnelley & Sons Company, Harrisonburg, Virginia

Reprinted by arrangement with Viking Penguin, a division of Penguin Books USA Inc.

To

Jon and Robert

CONTENTS

I.   *"Five Lire Times Forever"*   11

II.   *"Today! This Morning! This Very Second!"*   28

III.   *"You Can Sail Faster with Red Sails"*   43

IV.   *"The Most Beautiful Spot in All Capri"*   50

V.   *"A Long Story without an End"*   62

VI.   *"A Long Story without a Beginning"*   76

VII.   *"What Is So Difficult about an Egg?"*   97

VIII.   *"Eight Days!"*   118

IX.   *"I Didn't Say No"*   127

X.   *The End—and the Beginning*   138

RED SAILS TO CAPRI

I. "FIVE LIRE TIMES FOREVER"

"Angelo! Angelo, look! A boat!"

Angelo put down the net he was mending, pushed his red cap back off his forehead, and looked at Michele.

"A boat, eh? Wonderful! I must get excited. I must stop mending nets and stare. Here we sit on the island of Capri, with boathouses all around us, with fishing nets hanging like spider webs everywhere, with the bay full of boats which I've seen every day of my life for the past forty years—and the boy tugs at my arm, jumps up and down, screaming, and wants me to look. 'Look!' he says. 'Look, Angelo! A boat!' "

"But that's just it," cried Michele. "You don't see one like it every day of the year. It's different. It's—oh, look at it, Angelo, before it's gone. Why are you so stubborn? It will only take a minute."

"A minute, eh?" Angelo looked at Michele again, avoiding the sea as if it were against the law to look at it. "A minute! Listen to the boy! He speaks as if minutes grew on trees—thousands at a time. Minutes are not like that. They are all strung together in a straight line, holding hands, and if you lose one, it is gone, and—but no," he went on quickly, "now that I think about it I'm not so sure. There's your minute, and my minute, and our good friend Salaro over there, he has a minute which is different from ours. You know, I never thought about it before, but perhaps minutes are all spread out around us, like leaves and grains of sand."

"Angelo, do you know what people say about you?"

Angelo shook his head. "No, but I am sure of one thing: it is nothing good. Tell me, what do they say?"

"They say you are the laziest fisherman on Capri. They say you spend all your time talking, that you never do any-thing. *You* talk about minutes! They say you waste hours! Days! Years!"

Angelo nodded his head. "Forty," he said, looking

pleased. "Forty years I have wasted. It has been wonderful. Well, go on. Go on. What else do they say?"

"They say"—Michele hesitated—"they say—really, Angelo, I hate to say this, but it's true. They say"—he smiled at Angelo, as if to soften the blow—"they say you catch more fish than any other five fishermen put together."

Angelo laughed. "For that, Michele, I'll look at your boat, though really I don't like it. Staring at a boat like a landlubber! Like a foreigner! A tourist! Well, where is this boat you're so excited about? I've these nets to mend. I can't sit here all day looking at the sea."

"There!" Michele pointed to the left of the harbor. "Way out. You can just see the sails. Red ones. And look, Angelo! Look! It's coming into the harbor. It's going to land here!"

"Whee!" Angelo gave a low whistle. "By the good saints! That is a boat! But what is it doing in Capri this time of the year? It is cold now. The visitors stay away."

"Perhaps they aren't visitors."

"What else would they be? Do you know anyone on Capri who owns a boat like that?"

Michele shook his head slowly. "I didn't know anyone owned a boat like that anywhere."

"My poor little friend." Angelo patted Michele's arm. "When you have seen the world as I have, you will know that there are many sailboats even more beautiful than that."

"The world? Tell me, Angelo, where have you been?"

"To Naples."

Michele laughed. "Fifteen miles across the bay to Naples! My, Angelo, you have traveled!"

"Naples is a large city, and beautiful. You will do well to go there yourself someday."

Michele looked at the red sails, which were now quite close. "I'm going farther than Naples. I'm going to Rome. Perhaps even to Venice."

The red sails dropped, folding themselves around the masts. An anchor was lowered, and three men jumped out of the sailboat onto the Grande Marina pier.

"Beautiful!"

"*Beau! Très beau!*"

"Ah!"

Michele stared curiously at the three men. "What did they say, Angelo? Do you know?"

Angelo shrugged his shoulders. "I do not know. One thing is certain: they are not Italians."

"What do you think they are? You have seen many visitors. Can't you tell?"

"Well"—Angelo leaned forward and looked at them closely—"the first one, the one in the blue smock and tam, might be English. The one in the velvet breeches, the one who said, '*Très beau,*' he is French, I am almost sure. I used to know a bit of French. Let me see—*beau, beau.* I think that means beautiful. Yes, that is right. *Très beau*—very beautiful."

"What did they mean, Angelo? What is very beautiful?"

"Capri, of course. Did you think they meant you?"

"I am sure of one thing: they did not mean you."

"Then we are even."

"Even!" Michele laughed. "Now tell me about the tall blond fellow in the tight-fitting coat."

"Sh!" Angelo put his hand over Michele's mouth. "If you talked less, you would learn more. Listen! They're talking."

"And in Italian!" Michele pulled Angelo's hand away from his mouth. "They're speaking in Italian, and quite well too. I can understand them. Can't you, Angelo?"

"I could understand them if I could hear them," Angelo answered. "But, of course, with my young friend here, talk, talk, talking all the time—"

"And look"—Michele refused to be silenced—"they're taking baggage off the boat. It looks as if they're going to stay."

"Well?" Angelo looked at Michele. "Go! Quick!"

"Go? Me? Why?"

"The men! The men! Hurry!"

"The men?" Michele stared. "What have the men to do with me? Why can't I just stay here and look at them, like you? Like everyone else?"

Angelo shook his head. "The good saints help me! For a friend I have a *stupido,* dumb like a donkey. I must push him and pull him. I must draw pictures for him. I must ask him questions. Listen, Michele, where do you live?"

Michele looked back over his shoulder. The high rocks

that make up the center of Capri towered above him. Angelo could say that Capri was an island if he wanted to, but Michele knew better. It was a mountain, a sitting-down mountain with the village of Capri in its lap. The fact that there was water all around its feet didn't keep it from being a mountain.

"I live on a mountain." Michele grinned. It was an old joke between them.

"You live on an island." Angelo shook his head. "A piece of land with water all around it is an island."

"A piece of land that humps and rears and heaves is a mountain."

"All right! All right! You live on a mountain-island."

"I live on an island-mountain," Michele corrected him.

"All right! All right! But where? Where on this island-mountain do you live?"

"Up there." Once more Michele looked over his shoulder. "Up there, beyond the village, with my father and mother."

"And what does your father do?" Angelo asked the question in a high, sweet voice, as if Michele were one year old. Then, dropping two octaves, he barked the question again. "Tell me, quick! What does he do?"

Michele, amused, played the game with him. "He runs an inn," he answered, as if Angelo had not known him since the day he was born.

"Runs an inn, does he?" Angelo repeated. "Well! Well!

Well! And here are three strange men getting out of a boat with baggage and—"

"Angelo!" Michele jumped to his feet. "My father's inn has been closed for a month. He does not expect guests this time of the year. There will be nothing for them to eat. I must go quickly and tell him."

"So! You finally understand." Angelo smiled. "I was beginning to think you were going to stay here all day."

Michele made a wry face. "All right," he said, "I am not very smart—but you see I am smart enough to have a smart friend."

Angelo laughed. "And a generous friend too. Here, take this basket of fish to your mother. Then she will not have to worry about supper."

"Angelo—"

"Don't stop to thank me. It is nothing. Just go!"

Michele turned, then stopped again. "Signor Pettito's inn! Perhaps they will go there instead. One cannot be sure."

"Go! Go!" Angelo waved his arms. "Your friend who is smart and generous is also clever. They will go where I send them, and I will send them to your father's inn."

"You will send them? What makes you think they will listen to you?"

"Everyone listens to me."

Michele nodded. "When one talks all the time, someone is bound to hear."

"Go!"

"They will need donkeys to get to my father's inn."

"I shall arrange everything. Go!"

"Angelo"—Michele hesitated—"is it not strange that they come at this time of the year? Why do you think they have come?"

"To eat you alive, no doubt," Angelo shouted. "And if you don't hurry I'll beat them to it. Go! Go! Go!"

Half an hour later Michele stumbled into the courtyard of his father's inn. He had been running uphill steadily since he left the beach, scrambling over rocks and ledges, often on all fours, like some wild mountain animal. Now he stood leaning against a table, gasping for breath; his face twitched as sharp pains shot through his side.

"Michele!" Michele's mother, looking out of a window, saw him standing there. "Michele!"

Then, running through the house, she began to call, "Papa! Papa! Come quick! Something has happened!"

"Michele!" Signor and Signora Pagano reached the courtyard at the same time. "Michele! What is wrong? What happened?"

"He's ill! Look at him! He holds his side! He is in pain! Oh, my poor boy! My poor boy!"

"I'm not ill, Mamma, I—"

"You're hurt! That's it, you're hurt! How did it happen? Where? When?"

"I'm not hurt, Mamma!" Michele was still gasping for breath, and it was all he could do to talk. "Three men—"

"Three men!" Signora Pagano waved her hands in the air. "Bandits! Robbers! You were chased! But why? Why would they chase a fourteen-year-old boy? You have no money. Nothing! Why?"

"Mamma!" Signor Pagano patted his wife's arm. "Mamma, please! Don't get so excited. Let the boy talk."

"But he can't talk! Don't you see? He sits there panting like a fish that has been washed onto the shore."

Finally Michele found his voice. "I was down at the beach and—"

Signor and Signora Pagano looked at each other. Down at the beach! When wasn't Michele down at the beach? One might as well say the sky was blue, the grass green. Michele pretended not to see his parents' glances.

"—and a ship, a beautiful ship with red sails, came into the harbor, and three men—three strange men, with a great deal of luggage, got off—and Angelo—"

"Angelo! Humph!" Eager as she was to hear Michele's story, Signora Pagano could not resist showing her disapproval of Angelo. "Angelo! Always Angelo!"

"If it had not been for Angelo," Michele went on, "I might still be sitting there. It was he who made me realize, Papa, that these men, with so much luggage, would be wanting a place to stay."

"The good saints help us!" Signor and Signora Pagano looked at each other.

"There is no food in the house. Only a bit of macaroni for our own supper."

"The dishes, they will all be dusty, so long in the cupboard."

"The rooms! They will have to be aired!"

"I must go to the market!"

"Is it too cool to eat out here?" Signor Pagano waved his hands for a few minutes as if feeling the air. "Yes, too cool. We must eat inside."

"With a fire in the fireplace."

"Is there wood?"

"If only I had some fish!"

"Mamma!" Michele had forgotten the basket which was still on his arm. "Mamma, look!"

"Oh!" Signora Pagano looked into the basket. "Who sent them? The angel! The angel!"

Michele laughed. "It was an angel, Mamma. That's why they call him Angelo."

"Angelo? Angelo! He takes our son away from us and in exchange sends us a basket of fish. It is small pay. Small pay! But then one must be grateful." She sniffed at the fish to see if they were fresh.

Michele grinned at her, but his grin disappeared when the fish passed her approval and she handed the basket to him.

"All of the scales off, Michele. All of them. Not half of them, not some of them, not part of them, not most of them. All of them. All! And hurry. Papa will want you to open the three front rooms, and the floors must be swept."

Michele took the fish and started for the spring. He hated

to clean fish. The scales were terrible. They stuck to your hands and your clothing, and most of all to the fish themselves. He never got all of them, try as he would. Today, however, he worked faster and more carefully than usual. He did not want to be sent back to the spring to do the job over, nor did he want to be there when the men arrived.

Later he began to wonder why he had hurried so fast.

Three upstairs bedrooms had been opened, aired, and cleaned.

A big fire roared in the fireplace.

Lamps had been cleaned and lighted.

Furniture had been dusted, dishes had been washed.

Michele and his father, faces washed, hair combed, sat in the courtyard, waiting.

"There, there!" The words came from the kitchen along with a wonderful odor. "There, there! Cook slowly now. Do not hurry yourselves. The men have not arrived."

Signor Pagano looked at Michele and smiled. "Your mother," he said, "is a very remarkable person. Does she cook by recipe? No. Does she cook by taste? No. Does she cook by smell? No. Your mother, Michele, takes a few fish, and she talks to them, and argues with them, and scolds them, and flatters them, until finally she talks them into cooking the way she wants them. She takes a bit of dough and pats it, and teases it, and wraps it up in a cloth like a baby, and sings to it. Will she leave the kitchen when the bread is rising? No. And why not? Because the dough will not rise well by itself. It gets lonely. Bread lonely! Now I ask you? But what can I do? What can I say? Is she not the best cook in Capri?"

Michele swallowed hard and nodded. The odors from the kitchen were almost more than he could bear. Would the men never come?

"There, there!" Pots clattered. Lids were lifted and replaced. There was the sound of beating and scraping and stirring. "There, there! You would like some more lemon, yes? Good. But slowly now. Don't get too brown. The men have not come. There is much time."

There was too much time.

The sun began to set behind the mountains. Michele lighted more lamps, brought in more wood, and closed the shutters.

Still the men did not come.

Signora Pagano cooed to the fish, spoke harshly to the soup when it boiled over, and begged the figs to keep themselves juicy.

Finally she joined Michele and his father in the courtyard.

"Your three men," she said, looking at Michele, "where can they be? You are sure they will come? You heard them say so?"

"Well, no."

"*No!*" Signor and Signora Pagano stared at Michele.

"Well, not exactly."

"Not exactly? You did not hear them say they were coming here?"

"Not exactly."

"What did you hear them say?"

"They said that Capri was beautiful and—"

"Three strange men do not have to come in a wonderful boat with red sails to tell us what we already know," Signor Pagano interrupted. "Of course Capri is beautiful, and most beautiful of all at Signor Pagano's inn. But if they do not come—"

"They will come."

"Why are you so sure?"

"Angelo said—"

"Angelo!" Signora Pagano sniffed. "Always Angelo!"

"Oh, Angelo knows them?" Signor Pagano looked pleased. "That is good."

"No." Michele shook his head. "Angelo does not know them."

"Then how—"

"He said he would send them to us."

"And you believed him?" Signora Pagano put her hands up to her head and swayed back and forth. "How can you believe anything Angelo says? Don't you know he could not tell the truth if he had to? It is not that he has forgotten how. Oh, no. He never knew. Never! As a small child, a baby. Such stories! And now that he is grown he is much worse. Like all fishermen, he must make everything bigger and better than God intended it to be. Everything bigger and better. And he, Angelo, he makes the biggest and best of all. Angelo can do anything. Anything! He can even tell three strangers where to go, and they will obey him like little children. Because of him we have scrubbed and washed and cleaned and dusted. We have used olive oil and lemons and peppers and honey. All we had! A week's supply! We have upset the whole household, wasted wood and oil. And for what? For Angelo and his stories!"

Michele looked anxiously down the side of the mountain, then looked again. By leaning forward he could see six donkey ears moving across the top of a ledge. Six donkey ears meant that three donkeys must be walking on the path below, and it was reasonable to suppose that the donkeys belonged to Michele's good friend, Pietro, since young Pietro was also a friend of Angelo's, and Angelo would certainly call on Pietro if he needed three donkeys to bring the luggage of three strangers to Signor Pagano's inn.

"Mamma!" Michele sniffed the air. "Your fish! I can smell them. They must be burning!"

"My fish! My poor little fishes! I forgot all about them. Wait! Wait!" she cried. "I'm coming! I'm coming! Don't burn yourselves. I'm coming!"

Five minutes later, when Signora Pagano returned, the three men were just coming into the courtyard.

"Oh!" She stopped short and stared. "Oh!"

"I am sorry." The man in the velvet breeches, whom Angelo had said was probably from France, took off his cap and bowed. "I did not mean to startle you."

"Well, you see, I—I—I didn't—" Signora Pagano stopped, and Signor Pagano went on hurriedly, "My wife, Signora

Pagano, was surprised because—because—well, you see—"
Suddenly he began to smile. "You see, visitors do not usually
come to Capri this time of the year."

The man bowed again. "Good. That is just what we want.
No other guests. Peace and quiet." He looked around him,
then spoke to his two companions. "That fellow on the beach
—he was right. This is perfect. What was his name? I can't
remember. A charming fellow. Charming! Well, never
mind, I'll think of it." He turned back toward Signor and
Signora Pagano. "Let me introduce my companions: This
is Lord Derby, an English painter, who has come to Capri in
search of beauty. This is Herre Erik Nordstrom, a Danish
student, who has come to Capri to study all those books
which, I am afraid, are going to make that poor donkey over
there even more bowlegged than he was before. And myself,
Monsieur Jacques Tiersonnier—but you can forget my impossible last name; no one who has not been born in France
can ever pronounce it—and I, I am a writer who has come to
Capri in search of adventure."

Signor Pagano laughed. "There is plenty of beauty for
Lord Derby, and plenty of quiet for studying, but you,
Monsieur Jacques, I fear will be disappointed. Capri is a
peaceful little island, half asleep in the sun. I am afraid you
will not find this adventure you are seeking."

Lord Derby, who had been busy taking an easel off a
donkey, called back over his shoulder, "Do not worry, Signor
Pagano. When you have known Monsieur Jacques as long as
I have, you will know that if he does not find adventure,

adventure will find him. They were made for each other. When things happen, Monsieur Jacques is around. When Monsieur Jacques is around, things happen."

"Nothing too terrible, I hope," said Signora Pagano a little nervously.

"Don't worry," Monsieur Jacques whispered to her. "I am not as bad as they make me sound. Anyway, right now I think we are all most interested in searching for a bit of food." He sniffed the air. "Something smells heavenly. I think some good angel must have led us to this place." He clapped his hands together and began to laugh. "Now I remember that fellow's name. It was Angelo."

It took Pietro and Michele three trips each to get all the things upstairs. Books, boxes, easels, brushes, paints, chests, leather bags—there seemed to be no end to them. "Your poor donkeys," whispered Michele. "Will they ever be the same?"

Pietro laughed. "They will have the whole winter to straighten out their legs. As for me, it was a good bit of luck getting a few lire this time of the year. And you, Michele, you and your father and mother, are you not pleased? Is it not fortunate to have guests at this season?"

Michele nodded. "The winters are usually bad. Nothing to do and no money. I wonder how long they will stay?"

"Forever!" Pietro lowered a heavy chest to the floor. "With all this stuff they will stay forever, you can be sure. And if they stay forever," Pietro went on, pretending to figure on his fingers, "let's see, what does your father charge

a day, Michele, five lire? Let's see—five lire times forever—
why, Michele, you're rich. Rich! Rich!"

"Sh!" said Michele. "They'll hear you."

"Rich! Rich! Rich!" Pietro ran down the stairs. "Rich!
Rich! Rich! See you tomorrow, Michele."

"Tomorrow," Michele called after him, laughing. "Tomorrow."

II. "TODAY! THIS MORNING!
THIS VERY SECOND!"

"Michele?" Pietro called from the kitchen doorway. "Michele?"

"Yes?"

"May I come in?"

"Yes."

"Michele!" Pietro blinked. After walking for half an hour with the sun in his eyes, he found it difficult to see in the dark kitchen. "Michele, do you know what day this is?"

"Yes."

"But you forgot about it last night. I did too. The men coming and all the excitement—neither of us thought about it. But now it's here, Michele. The day we've been waiting for. Really here! Isn't it wonderful?"

"Pietro, I can't go."

"Can't go? Michele, are you ill?"

"No, I'm not ill."

"Then why?"

"Pietro, listen. These men who came last night, you saw

them, you know what kind of people they are. They're rich,
and they're used to a great deal of service. If they don't get it,
if everything isn't perfect, they won't stay. Their coming,
now, when we have no other guests, is a great blessing. Signor
Pettito would give his right arm to have them at his inn. And
you know Signor Pettito! He will do everything he can to
get them away from us. I have to stay here, Pietro. There is
so much to do. Already, and it is only eight o'clock, they have
called me six times. Lord Derby rang his bell for five minutes,
and when I finally got there, he wanted to tell me that he was
not to be disturbed. He sleeps late, he told me, and any dis-
turbance annoys him. I wanted to ask him if he had been
ringing the bell in his sleep, but I didn't. Monsieur Jacques
got up at five o'clock for a walk and wanted his breakfast *immediately*. Now there is lunch to fix, and food to buy for
dinner, and the rooms to clean. I can't go, Pietro, I can't."

Pietro sat as if he were turned to stone. Michele was not
sure he had heard a thing he said.

"Pietro."

"Yes?"

"You see, don't you? You see I cannot go?"

Suddenly Pietro jumped to his feet. "It's not fair. It's not
fair of your parents to keep you here. They know how much
this means to you. They should let you go. No matter what
happens, they should let you go."

Michele shook his head. "You don't understand, Pietro.
They want me to go. My father had tears in his eyes when he
talked to me this morning. But these men—if they had been

sent from heaven they could not have been more welcome. If they stay two weeks, we can paint the inn. Four weeks, and we can repair the patio. Six weeks—Pietro, if we could keep them for six weeks, my father says he could put some money away in the chest. Money in the chest, Pietro! Do you know what that means? When my grandfather lived there was money in the chest, but not since then. My father and mother have worked hard all their lives, but always there was never quite enough. For food, for clothing, to keep the inn—never quite enough. To have enough, and a bit left over—don't you see, Pietro, how wonderful that would be?"

Pietro's eyes flashed. "Why did they have to come this week? They could have come last week, or next week, or a year ago, or two years from now. Why did they have to come on November the first, 1826? We are fourteen years old, Michele, and in all those fourteen years there is one week when we can go to Naples. Six months ago Salaro said to us, 'The first week in November I go to Naples. Would you like to go with me?' Would we like to go with him! It is something we have dreamed about all our lives, and since Salaro asked us to go with him we haven't talked or thought about anything else. Who knows when we will ever get another chance? How many people on Capri have ever been to Naples? Has my mother? No. Has my father? No. Have your mother and father? N—"

"Yes."

"When?"

"They were born there."

Pietro nodded. "If you are poor and live on Capri, there are two ways to get to Naples. You can be born there or you can go with Salaro."

"Perhaps Salaro will go again."

"Go again?" Pietro laughed. "He has not been there for ten years, and he goes now only because his sister is getting married."

"Maybe he has another sister."

Pietro nodded. "Another sister named Margherita."

"Then perhaps Margherita will get married and he will go again."

"Fine! Splendid! We will wait for Margherita's wedding. She is beautiful and everyone loves her. There is only one thing wrong."

"Wrong?"

"Yes. There is one thing wrong. On her last birthday—"

"Yes, on her last birthday—go on."

"On her last birthday, my dear Michele, Margherita was four years old."

A bell began to ring upstairs, and Michele jumped to his feet. "Good-by, Pietro." He smiled. "Have a good time— good enough for both of us." He climbed a few steps and then looked down. "When you come back you'll tell me all about it, every minute, and—"

"Michele." Pietro looked up at him. "Michele, I'm not going. You don't think I'd go without you, do you?"

It was Michele's turn to stare. "Pietro, you can't mean it. It's—it's the most stupid, ridiculous, impossible—" The bell was ringing louder now, and Michele took another step. "Pietro, I can't argue now. I have to go. But you can't mean it. You can't. You have to go. Don't you see how I'd feel?"

"Michele, I'm not going. What fun would it be? We planned to go to Naples together, and when we go we'll go together, the way we planned."

The bell was being rung with both hands now. It clamored and clanked. "Pietro, please! You have to go. You—"

The bell had been thrown to the floor. It fell with a heavy thud and a small, whimpering tinkle. Michele gave Pietro one last desperate look and disappeared up the stairs.

"Pietro?"

Pietro swung around and saw Monsieur Jacques standing behind him. "Yes?"

"Where do you have to go, Pietro? Michele seemed very insistent."

"Nowhere."

"Nowhere?" Monsieur Jacques smiled. "That's a strange place to send a friend. Are you sure it doesn't have another name?"

Pietro shrugged. "Some people call it Naples."

"Naples?" Monsieur Jacques looked surprised. "Are you going to Naples, Pietro?"

"No."

"Why not?"

Pietro shrugged his shoulders again. "It's a long story. I have to go now, Monsieur Jacques. I—"

"Wait a minute, Pietro. When were you going to Naples?"

"This morning."

"With whom?"

"Salaro and—really I have to go, Monsieur Jacques, I—"

"With Salaro and Michele?"

Pietro nodded.

"And now Michele isn't going?"

Pietro nodded again.

"Why not?"

"Please, Monsieur Jacques. I—"

"Michele isn't going because we're here. Is that right, Pietro?"

Pietro's eyes flashed. "You shouldn't have made me tell you," he cried. "I didn't want to. I—"

"I know you didn't want to, Pietro, but this is a serious thing, a trip to Naples. How long have you planned it?"

"About six months."

"Six months, and now suddenly it's off. And all because of us." He sat down on the bottom step and pushed his cap off his forehead. "I know how you feel, Pietro. I know because I remember my first big trip. My family lived in a little village fifty miles from nowhere." He smiled. "You see I had a nowhere too, Pietro, and its other name was Paris. Paris! Whenever I said the word it was as if a whole orchestra were playing. It made me feel wonderful inside, just thinking about it. It made me feel rich and full and—well, juicy. Then one day my uncle had to go to Paris, and he took me with him. It was wonderful, Pietro. No trip I'll ever take as long as I live will be as wonderful as that first one. So you see how I feel, making you and Michele miss this chance." He looked at Pietro and smiled. "I don't suppose it would do any good if I offered to wash the dishes for Signora Pagano while Michele was away?"

"She'd die before she'd let you."

"I could break Lord Derby's arms so he'd stop ringing that bell."

Pietro laughed. "He'd find a way to ring it—with his teeth or his toes. It's no use, Monsieur Jacques. Michele won't go no matter what you do or say. And I won't go without him."

"Ah!" Monsieur Jacques looked up as Michele appeared at the top of the stairs. "Ah, Michele, you must help me. I have a problem."

"A problem, Monsieur?"

"Yes. Come down. Come down. I have a question to ask you."

"Yes?"

"If you were a man, Michele, a rather nice man, let us say; a man with a good heart, a man who liked to be happy and liked to see other people happy, and you had caused two boys to miss a trip to Naples, what would you do?"

"Pietro!" Michele stared at his friend. "Pietro, you didn't tell!"

"I tried not to tell him, Michele, really I did, but he kept asking me questions and putting words into my mouth. He wouldn't let me leave."

"Don't blame Pietro." Monsieur Jacques patted Michele's arm. "I made him tell me. Really I did. Anyway, I knew there was something wrong early this morning. A boy's face doesn't grow a foot longer overnight without a reason. Now let's see what we can do. Perhaps—hmmmmm. The island is called Capri, and this little village is called Capri too. Is that right?"

Michele nodded.

"Are there any other villages on the island?"

"One other. A village called Anacapri."

Monsieur Jacques laughed. "Someone certainly liked the name of Capri around here. Anacapri! 'Ana,' 'ana'—I believe that is a Greek word meaning up or upward. Is Anacapri up from here?"

"Up?" Both boys laughed. "Up? Would you say that seven hundred and eighty-four steps was up?"

"Seven hundred and eighty-four steps? Impossible! What does one see when one gets to the top?"

"The village of Anacapri."

"Is it worth it?"

Michele shrugged his shoulders. "It is all right."

"Nothing special?"

Michele shook his head.

"Too bad." Monsieur Jacques rubbed his forehead. "I thought perhaps we could go there today."

"Monsieur"—Michele hesitated— "Monsieur, I'm afraid

you don't understand. I can't leave the inn today. Naples, Anacapri—it doesn't matter."

"But if you went to Naples you would be gone a week. This would be only a part of a day."

Michele shook his head. "Even for a part of a day it is impossible. My father needs me here at the inn. Really, Monsieur, I am needed. He isn't being unreasonable. He wants to be sure that you and Lord Derby and Herre Nordstrom are happy and—"

"Ha! So I must be happy, must I? Whether I like it or not, I must be happy." Monsieur Jacques rubbed his forehead again. "Well, now, let's see. What would make me happy? Boys!" He put his arms around Michele and Pietro. "Boys, I have it. Michele, where is your father?"

"He was in the patio the last time I saw him."

"Good. Wait here. I'll be back in a few minutes."

As Monsieur Jacques left the kitchen Michele started up the stairs two steps at a time. "Come on." He waved to Pietro. "Come on. Quick! We can see and hear everything that goes on in the patio from the upstairs window. Hurry. I want to know what he's going to do."

The two boys leaned on the window sill. Michele was right. Monseur Jacques' words came up through the window as clearly as if he were talking to them instead of to Signor Pagano.

"Signor Pagano."

"Yes, Monsieur?"

"You were right."

"Right?" Signor Pagano looked pleased. It was nice to be told that one was right, especially by someone one wanted to please. "Yes, Monsieur Jacques?"

"Yes, Signor Pagano, you were right. You said last night that this was a quiet little village, half asleep in the sun. You were very right, Signor Pagano."

"You like our village, Monsieur?" Signor Pagano beamed.

"No."

The smile faded from Signor Pagano's face. "You are not pleased with it, Monsieur?"

"Not pleased a bit. On second thought, Signor Pagano, I don't think you were right after all. You said the village was half asleep. Look again, Signor Pagano. Look again. It is not asleep. It is dead, absolutely, impossibly dead. And I am bored."

"I am sorry, Monsieur."

"Signor Pagano, your being sorry does not help me. In fact it makes me more bored than ever. I like gay, happy people around me. I am bored with dead villages and sorry people. I think I shall leave tomorrow. No, tonight. I shall leave tonight."

"Oh, Monsieur, I'm sor—I mean—really, Monsieur, isn't there anything I can do?"

"Do? What is there to do? This place is all right for Lord Derby, who thinks only of beauty. He can go around ohing and ahing all day and be perfectly happy. And Herre Nordstrom—he sits with his nose in a book all day. He could be in a cave and not know the difference. But I, Signor Pagano, I must have some excitement. What is there to do around here?"

"You have not seen the island, Monsieur, or the village of Anacapri, up seven hundred and eighty-four steps, all hewed out of the rock. It is wonderful, Monsieur. There is nothing like it anywhere else in the world. Just think of it— seven hundred and eighty-four steps!"

"I don't want to think of it. It makes me tired just saying the number. Climb seven hundred and eighty-four steps? What do you think I am, a goat? A goat? That's it! A goat! I never thought of it before. Capri is a Latin word meaning goat. No wonder everything around here is named Capri. One must be a goat to live here, Signor Pagano. The men who discovered this place realized that. The island of Capri, the village of Capri, Anacapri. Capri, Capri, Capri—everywhere one turns. But I, Signor Pagano, am not, thank heavens, a goat; and not being a goat, I see no reason to spend any more of my time here on this mass of rocks."

"There is the water, Monsieur. Do you not like to swim?"

"Had God wanted me to climb mountains, Signor Pagano, he would have given me hoofs. Had he wanted me to swim, he would have given me fins."

"There are boats, Monsieur."

"Boats?"

"Yes, boats. Perhaps you would like to sail around the island. It is beautiful, I assure you. People come from all over the world just to make the trip. Surely you would not want to leave without seeing it."

"Well—"

"Could I get a sailboat for you, Monsieur?" Signor Pagano said eagerly. "There is one on the island for hire."

"I have my own boat, thank you."

"But you could not sail it alone."

"That is right. I would need some help."

"I could get someone to help you."

"Could you?" For the first time during the whole conversation Monsieur Jacques gave Signor Pagano an encouraging glance. "Could you? Someone who knows the waters? Someone who has spent a great deal of time on the beaches?"

"There is Riccardo."

"Riccardo?"

"A fisherman."

"I hate fishermen. They smell of fish."

"That is true, Monsieur." Signor Pagano tried to look patient. "Then there is Giulio."

"Giulio?"

"A sailor."

"I hate sailors."

"But, Monsieur—"

"I said, 'I hate sailors.' "

"Very well, Monsieur. Let's see. There is—Monsieur, I have it. The very one."

"Not a fisherman?"

"No."

"Not a sailor?"

"No."

"He knows the waters?"

"He lives in them."

Monsieur Jacques looked quizzical. "Not a fish?"

"Not a fish. Not a goat."

"Not a goat? Is his name Capri?"

Signor Pagano laughed. "No, not Capri."

"Good. All this place needs is a family by the name of Capri. I can just hear it. This is Signor Capri, who lives in the village of Capri, on the island of Capri. Every morning he goes up to Anacapri. This is his wife, Signora Capri, and his children, Mario Capri and Ferdinando Capri, and the baby, the joy of their life, they have named Capriccioso Capri."

Signor Pagano laughed. "You do not have to worry, Monsieur. This is a boy, and his name is Michele."

"Michele?" Monsieur Jacques looked surprised.

"You think he is too young?" Signor Pagano asked, looking worried.

"Perhaps."

"But really, Monsieur, I assure you he is not. He knows the waters better than anyone I know. He lives in them, swimming and sailing. There is not a rock or a reef he does not know. Even the ripples mean something to him. He reads them like a book. Really, Monsieur, you could not find a better guide on the whole island."

"Then why didn't you tell me about him at first?" Monsieur Jacques looked furious. "Why all those fishermen and sailors? Riccardos? Giulios?"

"Well," said Signor Pagano hesitantly, "you see, Michele,

for all his love of the water, is really a very good boy. Very good. He is a great help to his mother and me. A great help. And at a time like this, with guests to be taken care of—"

"You do not want him to go with me?"

"Oh, no, Monsieur, I do not mean that. I want more than anything else to make you and your friends happy. If taking Michele with you will make you happy, that is all that matters."

"I still think he might be a little young."

"Oh, Monsieur, I assure you."

"Perhaps if he had a friend, another boy, to go with us, I would feel a little better. Does he have a friend?"

"Yes, Monsieur, a very good friend. Pietro."

"Then I shall take him too."

Signor Pagano shook his head. "That is impossible."

"Impossible?"

"He has gone to Naples."

"To Naples?"

"This morning, early."

"But I saw a boy with Michele not five minutes ago. The donkey boy. Isn't that Pietro?"

"It is impossible." Signor Pagano started toward the kitchen. "But it might just be."

Michele and Pietro leaned back against the wall and looked at each other. "That boat!" Michele took a deep breath. "Have you seen it, Pietro? It is more wonderful than anything I've ever seen in all my life. I never dreamed I'd have a chance to sail in it. Pietro, this is better than going to Naples. Naples will wait for us, and anyone can walk on her streets, but when does a poor boy get a chance to set foot on a boat like that? When, Pietro?"

Pietro grinned. "Why, today, Michele. This very morning. This very second! Stupid! Come on. Can't you hear your father calling?"

III. "YOU CAN SAIL FASTER
WITH RED SAILS"

The boat was more wonderful than Michele had imagined. It was larger, cleaner, trimmer. The sails were redder.

"You like my red sails, yes?"

"Yes!" Never had there been a more enthusiastic answer to any question.

"You know why I have them?"

"Because they are beautiful?" Michele could not take his eyes away from them.

"Because you can see them from a great distance?" Pietro, too, looked at them appreciatively.

"Yes, yes. They are beautiful and seeable, but that is not all. It is a great secret. One I myself discovered. And as a special favor I shall tell it to the two of you." Monsieur Jacques put an arm around each of the two boys and drew them close to him. "A great secret. A great secret. You will promise never to tell?"

"Never!"

"Good. Then here it is." His voice dropped to a whisper,

though no one was within a hundred yards of the boat. "A great secret. A great discovery. *You can sail faster with red sails.*"

Both boys laughed. Monsieur was a wonderful fellow. It was a wonderful day. The sky and the water seemed made of one piece, and the red sails bellied against their blue.

You can sail faster with red sails!

Was it true? After half an hour Michele was ready to believe it. The boat skimmed across the water. It could have been a fish or a bird, or both. It was a new world for Michele and Pietro. They had never gone so fast before. Around them there was nothing but sun and wind, reds and blues.

Michele lay down on the deck and closed his eyes. "You can take all of the cities and throw them into the sea," he said slowly. "Nothing is as wonderful as this."

Monsieur Jacques smiled. "Nothing at all? Not even Naples?"

"Not even Naples."

Monsieur Jacques patted his shoulder. "You will not always think so, but I am glad you think so today. We will sail into that cove up ahead. We'll drop anchor there and look around."

Michele sat up and shaded his eyes with his hands. "Which cove did you say, Monsieur?"

"The big one almost at the end of the island. Right now the mountain above casts a shadow over it. Can't you see it?"

"I can see it." Michele's voice was flat. He looked at Pietro. "That is not a good place to drop anchor, Monsieur."

"Why not?"

"There—there might be hidden rocks just below the surface. It might be dangerous."

"Dangerous? It looks like the most peaceful spot we've passed."

"Monsieur, I beg of you, when we get close to the cove, make a wide semicircle around it. It is very dangerous."

"How wide?"

"At least a kilometer."

"A kilometer? But why?"

"It is best."

"Rocks? That far out?"

"There might be."

"There might be? Don't you know?"

"No one knows, Monsieur."

"What do you mean, 'No one knows'?"

"Just that, Monsieur."

"I don't understand."

"No one understands, Monsieur."

"No one understands? What are you talking about, Michele? What are you trying to tell me?"

"Monsieur, it is very difficult to understand. Perhaps you should wait and ask my father."

"But your father said that you knew more about this island and the waters around it than anyone."

"Perhaps, Monsieur, but no one knows about that cove over there."

"Why not?"

"It is a great mystery."

"A mystery? I like mysteries, Michele."

"Perhaps you wouldn't like this one."

"I have yet to see a mystery I have not liked. Tell me about it, Michele."

"Please, Monsieur. Wait and ask my father. I beg you." His face was grave, almost frightened.

"All right." Monsieur Jacques patted his arm. "All right. If that's the way you feel we'll forget about it. We'll pretend the cove isn't there, that we never saw it." He set the sails and made a wide semicircle around it. A few minutes later they had rounded the end of the island and were on the west side.

But nothing was quite the same. The sun wasn't as bright; the wind had died; even the sails seemed less red. It was as if they had taken the shadow which covered the cove along with them. It hung over the boat, over the sea and the sky, over their spirits.

Michele looked at Pietro. "It's always true, isn't it?"

"Always."

"We should have gone the other way around."

"I forgot about it. I forgot that everyone doesn't know."

"I did too."

"Well, it can't be helped now."

"No."

Their conversation died like the wind. There seemed to be nothing to say.

But when they reached the south side the wind came up

again and the sun was brighter. The cove seemed far away. Once more the boat skimmed across the water, and both boys regained their lost spirits.

"Well!" Monsieur Jacques smiled. "This is more like it. A dull boat on one's hands is bad enough; but a dull boat and two dull boys, no one deserves that."

Michele smiled. "I'm sorry, Monsieur. It's just—"

"Never mind. We've half the day left. I'm hungry. What do you say we pull in at the cove—" He stopped and looked at Michele questioningly. "Is that one ahead all right?"

Michele laughed. "That one is all right, Monsieur. They are all all right except—"

"Good. Now for some lunch, yes?"

The rest of the day was like the beginning. There was sun and wind, talk and laughter. The shadowy cove seemed far away.

It was late when they got back to the inn, and Signor and Signora Pagano were preparing supper.

Michele hurried toward the kitchen. Usually he did not like to help with the cooking, but tonight the warm room felt wonderful after the cool ocean air, and a dozen delicious odors rose from a dozen steaming pots.

"Michele!" Signora Pagano looked up. "You are just in time. Help Papa with the macaroni."

Michele tied a white apron around his middle and hurried to the stove. He was glad of a chance to talk to his father without being overheard.

"Papa?"

"Yes, Michele?"

"We went for a sail."

"I know."

"We passed the cove."

"The cove?"

"Yes."

Signor Pagano shrugged. "One always passes the cove on a trip around the island. It cannot be helped."

"But Monsieur Jacques—he wanted to stop there."

"What!" Signor Pagano put his hands to his head and rocked back and forth. "With a hundred coves around the island, why did he have to choose that one?"

It was Michele's turn to shrug. "I do not know. I only know that he did."

"What happened?"

"He wanted to stop there and have lunch."

"What did you say?"

"What could I say? First I said it was dangerous. But you know that cove—quiet and peaceful—and so he kept asking questions. Finally I said he should wait and ask you."

"Was he satisfied with that answer?"

Michele shrugged again. "Who can tell? I only know that he stopped asking questions. He was very kind and polite."

"Perhaps he will forget about it."

"Perhaps. Perhaps not."

"You don't think he will?"

"No."

Signor Pagano sighed. "Well, we shall see. We shall see."

"If he starts asking questions, what are you going to do?"

"Do? I do not know, Michele. I will have to worry about it when the time comes. Right now we must worry about something else. Those macaroni! If we ruin Mamma's macaroni—"

" 'Ruin my macaroni'!" Signora Pagano caught the last three words. "What are you two doing? Talk, talk, talking! Have I not told you about the macaroni? It is jealous! Jealous! If you do not watch it every minute, for spite it will boil over or get too soft or stick to the bottom. For spite! Because it is jealous! It wants all of your attention, all of your time, every minute! You must watch it, and look at it, and stir it, and admire it, otherwise— How many times must I tell you how it is with the macaroni?"

Michele smiled. The macaroni! What else was important? Questions? The cove? Even Monsieur Jacques! At the moment, in his mother's kitchen, nothing else was important.

The three of them flew about. Only the macaroni was calm. It had stuck to the bottom of the pan and was now bubbling quietly.

"See!" Signora Pagano nodded her head. "See what it did? And all for spite! Because it was jealous! What were you two talking about anyway?"

But Michele and his father were suddenly at the other end of the kitchen. They pretended not to hear.

IV. "THE MOST BEAUTIFUL SPOT
IN ALL CAPRI"

"Michele!"

Michele looked up. In the doorway stood an easel. Around and in front of the easel were rolls of canvas, bundles of brushes, a palette, old paint rags, two legs attached to a pair of boots, small paint pots, a wooden box, half a head of hair, one eye, part of a nose, and a thin cheek.

"Michele!"

The voice, at least, was not concealed. It came out from behind the easel, full and clear.

"Michele!"

"Yes, Lord Derby?"

The easel and everything attached to it moved a few steps closer. "Michele, may I borrow you for the day?"

"Borrow me?"

The easel could laugh as well as talk. "Yes. Monsieur Jacques borrowed you yesterday. I should like to borrow you today."

"Certainly, Lord Derby. What would you like me to do?"

"I want to paint—up in the mountains. Do you know a place that is especially beautiful?"

"The most beautiful spot in all Capri."

"Good."

"It is not easy to get there."

"That doesn't matter."

Doesn't matter! Michele looked toward the doorway. Already he could feel the easel beating against his legs, the paint pots knocking against his side, the weight of the wooden box upon his head.

The easel started to turn around, then swayed dangerously. Michele sprang forward. "May I help you, Lord Derby? Shall I carry your things?"

The half-head of hair, the eye, the part of a nose, the thin cheek moved from side to side. "No. No, thank you, Michele. I always carry my things myself. Foolish of me, I know. You'll have to excuse a fussy old artist."

Excuse! Michele ran off to the kitchen to hide his face. The beating legs of the easel, the knocking paint pots, the heavy box had been lifted from him. He felt as free as the wind—but not for long.

"Yes, yes." Signora Pagano nodded her head. "Certainly you may go, Michele. We must do everything we can to keep the guests happy. You will be gone all day? That will mean lunch." She began, hastily, to put things into a basket.

Michele groaned. His mother lived with the constant fear that everyone around her was going to starve to death, and her whole life was spent in trying to avoid that great tragedy.

"Mamma," Michele could not keep from protesting, "Mamma, we will be gone only a day."

"To have a little extra food along is always a good idea. You can never tell what might happen."

"What could possibly happen?"

"You can never tell."

"Do you think we are going to get lost?"

"You lost on Capri?" Signora Pagano smiled.

"Bitten, perhaps, by a snake?"

"There are no snakes on Capri."

"Break an ankle?"

"The good saints help us!"

"Fall down a cavern?"

Signora Pagano could stand no more. "All right! All right! Here!" She covered the basket with a clean cloth and handed it to Michele. "Go, and careful now. Careful!"

Careful! She should have seen the basket half an hour later. First it swayed dangerously on top of Michele's head. Next it hung by a thin cord from his shoulder. It was thrown, half tipping, across small streams.

Halfway up a hill Michele looked back at Lord Derby, who was walking behind him. He looked like a paint shop on two legs. "Are you all right, Signore?"

"I suppose so." Lord Derby stopped to catch his breath. "How much farther, Michele?"

"One more hill after the steps."

"The steps?"

Michele pointed straight ahead. "Look!"

"By Jove!" Lord Derby stared. "I've seen steps in my life, Michele, but never any to compare with those. One cannot see the top."

"While you climb them you are sure there is no top."

Lord Derby looked at Michele questioningly. "You do not sound too fond of them."

"I hate them."

"Hate them?"

"Yes."

"Why?"

"I think they're ugly. They break your back with their steepness, blister your feet with their hardness, hurt your eyes with their glaring. They are like a great scar on the side of the mountain."

"Where do they go?"

"To Anacapri."

"Are we going to Anacapri?"

"No. Not if you want to see what I think is the most beautiful spot on the island."

"All right, Michele. Someday I shall ask you to take me to Anacapri, but not today. Let's see that favorite spot of yours."

Michele found an opening between two tall bushes. "This way, Signore. Here is our path."

"Our path!" Lord Derby laughed. "It might be your path, Michele, but it isn't mine. I can't see a path any place."

"What?" Michele looked down at his feet. "You can't

see it? It is plain as day to me. Beneath the leaves and the underbrush—"

"Paths that are beneath leaves and underbrush are not as plain as day."

Michele laughed. "Never mind. Just follow me. It is not far. Only a few steps. We are almost to the top."

One moment they were surrounded by trees and bushes. The next moment the whole world seemed made of nothing but sea and sky and high stone cliffs.

"Ah!" Lord Derby looked around him. "I understand now, Michele."

"Understand?"

"Yes. This place is not real. That is why one must follow an invisible path to reach it. Nothing as beautiful as this could be real. Some good genii— How long do I have before the genii take this away? How long before it vanishes?"

Michele rubbed his chin thoughtfully. "Well, let me think." His eyes twinkled. "It will not vanish, I promise you, Lord Derby, until the sun disappears behind that farthest cliff."

"Good, good! Then I have all day." In a few minutes the easel was set up and the canvas stretched across it. The paint pots were opened.

"Michele?"

"Yes, Lord Derby?"

"What are you going to do?"

"You mean now?"

"Yes."

"Why, nothing, Lord Derby. Just wait here until you are ready to go home."

"Then will you talk to me? I like to talk while I paint."

Michele sat down beneath a tree and crossed his legs. He squirmed around for a few minutes; then he smiled uncertainly. All morning he had talked to Lord Derby. Now, suddenly, when he was asked to talk he could think of nothing to say.

Lord Derby put a bit of paint on a brush and dabbed at the canvas. "Tell me about yourself, Michele. What do you do? Who are your friends? Do you get lonely up there at the inn?"

"Lonely? Never lonely. There is so much to do. Pietro and I—"

"Who is Pietro?"

"Pietro is the donkey boy. He is my best friend." Then, quickly, Michele added, "Angelo is my best friend too."

Lord Derby looked up. "You are fortunate, Michele. Most people are lucky to have one best friend. To have two—"

Michele nodded. He was well aware of his good fortune. To have Pietro and Angelo both was more than anyone deserved.

Lord Derby looked out across the water. He looked so long and so hard Michele thought he had forgotten about everything, including his painting. Suddenly he began to paint again, furiously, with short, quick strokes.

"Angelo." Lord Derby repeated the name slowly. "Isn't that the fellow we met on the beach? Tell me about him, Michele."

Michele laughed. How could one tell about Angelo? "Well," he began, "he is a fisherman."

"A fisherman. Yes?"

"He's—he's about forty years old."

"Forty years. All right, go on, tell me more."

"He lives by himself in a little cottage close to the sea."

"All of this tells me nothing about your friend Angelo."

"I know, I know." All at once the words were there. Michele could not say them fast enough. "Angelo is wonderful. Next to my father he is the most wonderful man in all the world. He's always laughing and singing. When you are with him you feel good inside. Everything is important to Angelo. Everything! The color of a fish. The way he ties a knot. The way he mends a net. The way he wears his hat on his head. Everything is important. And nothing is important. Nothing! He laughs at everything. And his stories—he tells wonderful stories. My mother doesn't like him."

Lord Derby didn't take his eyes off his painting. "Why doesn't your mother like him?"

"She says he doesn't tell the truth, that he doesn't know how, that he twists and turns everything. What do you think, Signore? Do you think it is wrong of Angelo—wrong of Angelo"—Michele hesitated and then went on—"do you think it is wrong of Angelo not always to tell the truth?"

Lord Derby sat with one brush between his teeth, six

clutched in his left hand, and one in his right. Finally he took the brush out of his mouth and put it behind his ear. "I don't know, Michele. I'm afraid I can't answer that question. But let me tell you this. I think that almost everyone is looking for something—something special, something that means more to him than anything else in the world. Do you remember the first night we came to the inn? Monsieur Jacques said that I had come to Capri in search of beauty and that he had come in search of adventure."

Michele nodded.

"But it is not just in Capri, Michele, that we do our searching. I look for a bit of beauty no matter where I go, and Monsieur Jacques is forever searching for adventure. And we find it, Michele. I think some way or other most people find the things they look for. Perhaps your friend Angelo is searching for gaiety, Michele. He must find something to laugh about, something to make others laugh. When he doesn't find it he makes it up. That's his way of finding what's important to him. That doesn't seem too wrong to me."

Michele nodded. He wasn't quite sure he understood what Lord Derby was saying, but it was right to say that Angelo searched for gaiety—and that he found it. He wondered what he would search for when he was grown.

"Lord Derby?"

"Yes, Michele?"

"Does everyone search for something?"

"Almost everyone, I think."

"Even Herre Nordstrom?"

Lord Derby laughed. "I'm not sure about him, Michele. I think perhaps he is one person who hasn't found anything to look for. That is why he keeps himself buried in his books."

Lord Derby threw a large cloth over his canvas. "What do you say, Michele? Let's have lunch, take a small nap—"

"A nap! I never sleep in the daytime."

When Michele awoke, Lord Derby was painting again. "Well!" He looked at Michele and smiled. "For a boy that never sleeps in the daytime you are a good actor."

Michele grinned sheepishly. "I was just watching the clouds, and then the next thing I knew it was now."

"You awoke just in time. I have finished my picture. Do you want to see it?"

Michele started toward the picture, but Lord Derby stopped him. "Wait a minute. If you like the picture I'll give it to you. But you must tell the truth."

Michele looked around him. How wonderful it would be to take this place home with him—the sea and the sky and the cliffs! He walked to the front of the easel, looked at the canvas, then looked again.

There was no sea, no sky, no cliffs.

"The steps," he gasped. "You painted a picture of the steps to Anacapri."

Lord Derby nodded, well pleased with himself. "Do you like my picture?"

Michele nodded slowly. "Yes. Only—"

"Only what?"

"The steps are so beautiful."

"Have I made them too beautiful? More beautiful than they really are?"

"I never thought they were beautiful at all. I thought they were ugly."

"Perhaps you have never looked at them before."

"Looked at them? I have looked at them a thousand times."

"Sometimes we never look at the things we see most often."

Michele continued to stare at the picture. "Those colors in the rocks—are they really there?"

"I saw them there."

"And the steps—do they loop and turn like that?"

"Exactly like that."

"You have made them look like a stairway to heaven!"

"Have I? Good. It should be easy to climb a stairway to heaven, eh, Michele?"

But as they walked toward home Michele was still puzzled.

"Lord Derby."

"Yes, Michele."

"Why did you go to the most beautiful spot on Capri and then paint something else?"

"Your spot was too beautiful, Michele."

"Too beautiful?"

"Yes. I don't believe there is enough paint in the world

to paint a picture of that spot as it should be painted. At least I am not good enough to do it. But that doesn't worry me. You don't need an artist to show you the beauty of a place like that. But your ugly steps—if I have made you see a bit of beauty in them, Michele, I am very happy."

They were almost home when they saw Herre Nordstrom walking along the path.

"Well," Lord Derby greeted him enthusiastically, "it's good to see you out of doors. I was beginning to think you'd never leave your books long enough to see anything of this beautiful island."

Herre Nordstrom looked a little embarrassed. "I know you think I'm nothing but a bookworm, but there is so much to learn. Philosophy is a big subject."

"Philosophy." Michele repeated the word to himself. He had never heard it before. He listened while Lord Derby and Herre Nordstrom talked. "Philosophy." The word was repeated again and again.

When they got close to the inn Lord Derby sat down on a large boulder. "I'm going to rest here awhile," he said, "and watch the sun set. You two go on. I'll see you at dinner."

"Philosophy." Michele said the word carefully to himself. He was afraid he would forget how to pronounce it.

"Herre Nordstrom?"

"Yes, Michele?"

"May I ask you a question?"

"Certainly."

"What does philosophy mean?"

Herre Nordstrom stopped walking and stood very still in the middle of the path. "It means—" He laughed as if he were embarrassed. "Let's see, how can I explain it to you. Philosophy is a search for the truth through knowledge. Yes, that's it. All philosophers search for the truth. Do you understand, Michele?"

Michele shook his head. "No, Herre Nordstrom, I don't understand, but I am pleased about one thing."

"What's that, Michele?"

"Lord Derby said you hadn't found anything to look for. But you have, haven't you? You're searching for something, just like everyone else."

Herre Nordstrom smiled. "That's right, Michele, but I have chosen a difficult thing to search for, so difficult I cannot even explain it to you."

"That's all right, Herre Nordstrom. Don't worry about it. Perhaps some day, when I am older."

"Perhaps, Michele."

V. "A LONG STORY WITHOUT AN END"

If the sirocco hadn't started it might never have happened. But the sirocco did start, and when the sirocco blows, people do queer things. A sirocco is a wind—but not an ordinary wind. It is a wind laden with dust that sends everyone indoors and keeps them there.

The days seemed endless. Lord Derby stared moodily out of the windows. Monsieur Jacques paced the floor like a caged animal. Only Herre Nordstrom seemed not to mind. He sat in a corner, his head bent over his books.

By the second evening everyone was restless. They sat— the three guests and the three Paganos—around the big fireplace, trying to keep warm. Now and then someone would try to start a conversation, but it never lasted long. It was hard to compete with the howling wind which seemed to grow louder every second. Finally, after a particularly long silence, Monsieur Jacques looked up. "Signor Pagano," he said, "I just happened to think of something. You know the second day I was here I went for a sail with Michele and Pietro."

"Yes, Monsieur Jacques, I remember."

Michele held tight to the arms of his chair. He knew what was coming.

"While we were sailing," Monsieur Jacques went on, "we passed a little cove. I wanted to drop anchor there and have lunch, but Michele wouldn't let me. He said it was dangerous. But when I asked him in what way it was dangerous, he wouldn't tell me. Finally he told me to wait and ask you."

Signor Pagano shifted uneasily in his chair. "It is a long story, Monsieur Jacques, and it has no end."

Monsieur Jacques laughed. "It is a long evening, Signor Pagano, and it too seems endless. Perhaps this night and your story were made for each other."

The wind howled around the inn and beat against the windows. Signor Pagano nodded. "Perhaps you are right. If I must answer your question sometime, and I suppose I must, this is a good night to do it. At least we need not fear that someone will hear us. Before I start, I must ask you to promise that you will never repeat anything I tell you this evening."

Monsieur Jacques and Lord Derby nodded. Herre Nordstrom nodded too, but no one could tell whether he was nodding over a passage that pleased him in one of his books or whether he, too, was willing to promise.

Everyone moved a little closer to Signor Pagano, for his voice was low, and it was difficult to hear him above the roaring of the wind.

"First," he began, "there are a few facts you must know in order to understand some of the things I'm going to tell

you. I believe I have mentioned that Signora Pagano and I
are not natives of Capri. We were born in Naples and lived
there until we were married, fifteen years ago. I come from a
long line of innkeepers, and when someone told us that Capri
had only one inn, and was badly in need of another, we decided to come here and open one of our own. The inn was
needed, there was no doubt of that, and life should have been
easy for us. But it wasn't. Half of Capri is related to Signor
Pettito, who owns the other inn, and they lined up, like an
army, to protect him. From the minute a tourist got off of the
boat he heard nothing but *Signor Pettito*. Every small
boy, every market woman, every sailor on the beach, when
asked about a place to stay, would answer, '*Signor
Pettito*.' I was sometimes surprised that they didn't teach
the donkeys that carried the luggage to bray it too. Perhaps
they tried and couldn't. In any case, Signor Pettito's inn had
to be so crowded that guests were hanging out of the windows
before any happened to land up here. Not that anyone ever
mentioned our inn. Unthinkable! But sometimes people happened to wander up here and were pleased to find a place that
was quiet and peaceful.

"Now you must understand," Signor Pagano went on,
"that all of this didn't happen because the people of
Capri disliked us. Not at all. But our grandfathers weren't
born on Capri. Our fathers weren't born on Capri. And
—an unbelievable thing—we ourselves weren't born on
Capri. We were foreigners! We had come all the way from
Naples, fifteen miles across the bay! If we spoke a different

language, wore different clothes, ate different food, it could not have been worse. We were strangers—and what were strangers doing on Capri? Today, after fifteen years, we have many friends. The people of Capri like us. They are kind and generous. But we are still foreigners. Yesterday there was a meeting of the men of Capri. The market place must be moved and we are trying to decide where to move it. About halfway through the meeting I offered a suggestion. Everyone stared at me. What right had I, a foreigner, to tell these natives of Capri what to do? And that after fifteen years!" Signor Pagano shook his head.

"However," he went on, "we have made progress. Last summer a cousin of Signor Pettito's recommended our inn to a tourist. True, he had had a fight with Signor Pettito the night before, but two, three years ago that would not have made any difference. He would have recommended the inn of a cousin he hated long before he would have recommended the inn of a foreigner whom he liked." Tears came to Signor Pagano's eyes. "Slowly, through the years, we have worked our way into this little island. Today many have forgotten that we were not born here. I want you to know, Monsieur Jacques, Lord Derby, Herre Nordstrom"—Herre Nordstrom looked up from his book, smiled absent-mindedly when Signor Pagano mentioned his name, and then went on with his reading—"I want you to know it and understand it and accept it. Otherwise you will not be able to understand the other things I am going to tell you."

Signor Pagano moved a little closer to the fire. Everyone

else moved a little closer too—everyone, that is, except Herre Nordstrom. He stayed in his corner, his book open on his lap.

"Shortly after we came to Capri," Signor Pagano went on, "an old fisherman, a kind, friendly fellow, asked me to go with him on a trip around the island. I too, Monsieur Jacques, saw the cove you mentioned, and I too thought it looked inviting. But when I mentioned it to my friend—the good saints help us! I thought the boat would turn over with his ravings. 'Never mention that cove to anyone,' he shouted to me. 'Never! Do you understand? Nothing will mark you as a foreigner so quickly. Nothing! If you want to live in peace, forget about the cove. I am your friend, Signor Pagano,' he said to me, 'and I tell you this as a friend. Promise me you'll never mention the cove again. It is bad luck, believe me. The worst of bad luck.'

"I wanted to ask him to explain. A thousand questions came to my mind. But he was so upset, and I was so surprised by his sudden outburst, I could think of nothing to say. I shrugged my shoulders and nodded my head. My one thought was to calm him. 'I promise,' I kept saying. 'I promise.'

"My words seemed to quiet him. 'Good,' he said, giving me a friendly pat. 'You are a smart man, Signor Pagano. You learn quickly. You will go far.'

"But," Signor Pagano went on, "my shrugging and my nodding and my smiling were all on the outside. Inside I was burning with curiosity. What could be so terrible about a peaceful little cove? What had happened there? What might happen? Who could tell me?

"Many nights I lay awake thinking about it. I would become excited, furious. I would make up my mind, first thing in the morning, to find out the secret of this silly, impossible, ridiculous, terrible thing. But always, in the morning, I would remember how my friend had acted when I spoke of the cove. I remembered I had promised not to mention it again. And most of all I remembered his words, 'Nothing will mark you as a foreigner so quickly.' So, always, I was afraid to ask my questions.

"This went on for years, and then"—Signor Pagano smiled—"then—well, I suppose I finally did become a native of Capri. For me the cove ceased to exist. I haven't thought about it for years. It is easy to forget it. I have sat, time after time, and watched boats make a wide semicircle around it. I have seen sailors and fishermen cross themselves when they pass it. But in the fifteen years I have lived here I have never heard anyone mention it."

Signor Pagano stopped talking, and for a while everyone was silent.

Finally Monsieur Jacques spoke. "Signor Pagano, my friends say if I don't find adventure, adventure will find me. I think your little island has just been waiting for me to come along and discover its secret."

Signor Pagano turned pale. "Monsieur Jacques, perhaps you have forgotten. Before I started my story I asked you to make a promise. You promised not to repeat anything that was said here tonight. Surely you are a man of your word."

"I am indeed, Signor Pagano, and I understand perfectly why you have kept silent all these years. I know how important your silence has been to you and your family. But surely I, a total stranger, could ask a few questions without hurting anyone. I—"

Signor Pagano stopped him. "First, Monsieur Jacques, let me say this. Your questions will do you no good. You can ask questions for a week, for a month, for a year, and you will know no more in the end than you know at this minute. Your questions will be met with icy stares, with a shrug of the shoulders, with a small laugh, an arched eyebrow—and with complete silence. There is something which I suppose I have not made clear. The natives of Capri think it is bad luck even to mention the cove. Why should they run the risk of bringing bad luck to themselves in order to satisfy a stranger? Remember, then, your questions will do you no good. And remember this too. Your questions will do me almost as much harm as if I asked them myself. You, as you say, are a stranger here. You have scarcely spoken to anyone except the five of us. What, then, will happen if you start suddenly to ask questions? I have, as I said, many friends here. But I have some enemies too. Signor Pettito, as I have mentioned, is not overly fond of me. What would happen if he should begin asking a few questions himself? 'Why,' he could say, 'is Signor Pagano's guest so interested in a certain little place on this island?' He will not mention the cove, you may be sure, but everyone will know what he means.

"Before long everyone will be sure that I have put you up to it. A few more questions from Signor Pettito and they will be sure that I brought you all the way from France for that very purpose. First thing you know they will be calling you a spy—a foreign spy. The next thing you know—" Signor Pagano shrugged his shoulders. "As you yourself have said, Monsieur Jacques, there is not much to do in Capri. The evenings are long and the wine is strong. It is easy to put ideas into people's heads when they have nothing else to think about. A little excitement is pleasant and welcome. Everyone adds a bit to the story to make it more interesting. Who knows where it might end?"

Monsieur Jacques walked back and forth across the room. Finally he stopped in front of Signor Pagano. "It is not easy," he said, "to give up a chance for adventure, but perhaps you are right."

Once more everyone was silent.

Then, "Wonderful!" The word rang out in the quiet room. A book slammed shut with a heavy clap. "Perfect!"

The book fell to the floor and Herre Nordstrom strode across the room. "Unbelievable!"

Five pairs of eyes stared at Herre Nordstrom. What had happened to him? Where was his shyness, his quietness? Where were his low voice, his dreamy eyes, his absent-minded look? He seemed taller now. His voice rang out, full and deep. His cheeks were flushed.

"Michele," he said. "Do you remember when you asked me the meaning of philosophy?"

"Yes, Herre Nordstrom."

"You didn't understand what I told you?"

"No, Herre Nordstrom, I'm afraid I didn't."

"That worried me, Michele."

"Worried you, Herre Nordstrom?"

"Yes. For years I have studied philosophy. I was sure I knew a great deal. I was pleased with myself. I thought I was a great scholar. But when you asked me a simple question I couldn't give you a simple answer that you could understand. Suddenly I was all tangled up in words. What good, I asked myself, did all my learning do me? I was very unhappy. But now everything is all right again. I have found a way to explain what I meant to you. It is very simple." Herre Nordstrom smiled to himself.

Suddenly Signor Pagano looked happy too. The evening had not turned out badly after all. Monsieur Jacques seemed satisfied about the cove, and now here was Herre Nordstrom turning the conversation to something entirely different. Philosophy! Signor Pagano smiled. He knew no more about it than Michele, but he was sure of one thing: it was a nice, safe subject. He hoped they would talk about it the rest of the evening.

"Come, Herre Nordstrom." Signor Pagano thumped him on the back. "Come, tell us about it. We are all interested."

Herre Nordstrom was pleased with Signor Pagano's interest. "Really," he said, "it is unbelievable to find something so perfect."

"What is perfect, Herre Nordstrom? Come, come. We are eager to hear."

"The cove."

"What has the cove to do with philosophy?"

"It is perfect."

"Perfect?" This time Signor Pagano's voice showed nothing but disapproval.

"Yes." Herre Nordstrom turned away from Signor Pagano and put his arm around Michele's shoulders. "Do you remember, Michele, I said that all philosophers search for the truth through knowledge? I was talking about ideas, but ideas or coves—it is all the same. Now here is a cove and we want to find out the truth about it. How will we find the truth? Through knowledge. And how will we get the knowledge? By going to the cove. See how simple it is?"

"Simple?" Signor Pagano's eyes were flashing. "Herre Nordstrom, I'm afraid you didn't understand. To go to the cove is impossible."

"Why?"

Signor Pagano was really angry now. "Why? Why? Herre Nordstrom, all evening you sat with your nose in a book. It takes a brilliant man to read with his eyes and listen with his ears to two different things at the same time."

Herre Nordstrom bowed. "Thank you, Signor Pagano."

"It was not intended for a compliment."

"But I accept it as one. I, Signor Pagano, heard every word you were saying all evening."

"If you did you would not stand there asking foolish questions."

"I do not think my questions are foolish. Why can't I go to the cove?"

"How do you think you are going to get there?"

"I will hire someone to take me."

"No one will even mention the cove. How can you possibly think that anyone will take you there?"

"Then I shall go by myself."

"How?"

"In a boat."

"Where will you get one small enough to enter the cove?"

"I'll buy one."

"Where?"

"Here, on Capri."

"There are no boats for sale on Capri."

"Then I'll get a fisherman to sell me one."

"No one will sell you his boat."

"Why not?"

"Why should a fisherman sell his boat?"

"I will pay him well."

Signor Pagano laughed. "When you buy a fisherman's boat, Herre Nordstrom, you must buy many things: his boat, the fish he will catch, his love of the sea, the feel of the wind in his face, the excitement, the danger, his pride in the haul. It is a big price, Herre Nordstrom."

"He could buy himself another boat."

"Where?"

"Here, on Capri."

"They do not make boats on Capri."

"In Naples then."

"How would he get to Naples?"

"In a boat."

"What boat? He has no boat now. He has sold it to you."

"Someone else could take him."

"Who?"

"A friend of his, another fisherman."

"And miss a week's fishing? Why should he?"

"I would pay him well."

"What? You wish to buy two boats, Herre Nordstrom? Two fishermen? Two catches? Two loves of the sea? Two winds? Two excitements? Two dangers? Two prides? You are richer than I thought, Herre Nordstrom."

Herre Nordstrom shrugged. "All right! All right! Then I won't buy a fisherman's boat. But I'll get one some way, if I have to go to Naples myself and buy one."

"You are a fool!"

"Why?"

"With thousands of coves, why do you have to worry about this one? We don't bother the cove, the cove doesn't bother us. It is a good arrangement."

"But the cove does bother me. I want to find out the truth about it."

"You are risking your life for something that is not important."

"It is important to me."

"Important enough to die for?"

"No one is sure I am going to die."

"There is a saying, Herre Nordstrom: 'Where there's smoke, there's fire.' When people are afraid of something there must be a reason."

Herre Nordstrom's eyes flashed. "I don't believe that. People are afraid of anything they don't understand. When they understand, when they know the truth, they can do something about it. Look at Columbus. Everyone told him he would drop off the edge of the earth if he sailed too far, but he sailed on anyway. If he had listened to that kind of talk he would never have discovered America."

Signor Pagano laughed. "Don't fool yourself, Herre Nordstrom. You'll make no great discovery. You'll find no 'America' in the cove."

"Columbus wasn't searching for America, he was searching for the truth—the truth about the world."

"That may well be true, Herre Nordstrom, but this is true also. I have lived among fishermen and sailors all my life and I have learned many things. Most important, I have learned this: fishermen and sailors are not easily fooled. The sea is their life—and their death. They know when to have courage and when to be afraid. They have many superstitions, but you can be sure of this: there is a good reason behind every one. You will do well to respect them."

"I too know a saying, Signor Pagano. It goes like this: 'Finders keepers. Losers weepers.' All my life I've tried to find the truth with words. Now I have a chance to find it with action. And I am not going to lose that chance, Signor Pagano. No matter what happens, I am not going to lose that chance."

Then, without another word, Herre Nordstrom left the room.

"Whee!" Monsieur Jacques gave a low whistle.

Signora Pagano crossed herself. "May the saints help us!"

Lord Derby walked back and forth across the room. "Too much learning," he muttered to himself, "too little sense."

Signor Pagano looked dazed. "The longer I live," he said slowly, "the less I know. He is the last person in the world I would have expected to cause any trouble. All day he sat buried in his books. He seemed afraid of his own shadow, of his own voice. But now—now!"

"It's all my fault, Papa. It's all my fault," said Michele dolefully.

"Why, Michele? Why is it your fault?"

"Well, you see, if I hadn't asked him the meaning of philosophy—"

Signor Pagano gave a short laugh. "Well, Michele, it can't be helped. Who would think that a simple question would set him off like that?" Suddenly he remembered how angry he was. "Bah! That young jackanapes! Going to teach us the meaning of philosophy, is he? Doesn't care how much trouble he stirs up—doesn't care what happens to anyone! Well, he might learn a thing or two himself!" Signor Pagano nodded slowly. "Yes, he might learn a thing or two himself before it's all over."

VI. "A LONG STORY WITHOUT A BEGINNING"

It was scarcely light when Michele left the inn the next morning. The mountain paths and the village streets were deserted. The beach was deserted too, and the ocean—no, not the ocean. The ocean had one small boat on it, and a small speck inside the boat.

"Angelo, Angelo!" Michele ran across the sand. "Angelo, wait!"

With every step the speck grew larger. It had a head now, and arms. It waved an oar.

"Angelo!" Michele was panting when he finally reached the boat. "Angelo, I was afraid I'd miss you."

"One more wave and you would have. I was just ready to leave." Angelo looked pleased. "You're going fishing with me?"

"No, Angelo. No, I can't. I left the inn before anyone was awake. No one must know I have come. I must hurry back. I—oh, Angelo!"

"What is the matter, Michele?"

"A dreadful thing has happened. Dreadful!"

"What?"

"Angelo, what do you really think about the cove?"

"The cove?"

"Yes."

"Why do you ask?"

"Angelo, listen." In a few minutes Michele told all that had happened the night before.

Angelo shook his head. "It is a bad business, Michele. A bad business."

"I know. I—Angelo, you know what will happen if Herre Nordstrom insists upon going? The whole town will blame Papa because he is a guest at our inn. They'll blame Papa for any bad luck that happens to anyone for years to come."

Angelo nodded.

"Angelo?"

"Yes, Michele?"

"Angelo, are you afraid of the cove?"

"Afraid? Me? Do you not know? Angelo is afraid of nothing." He winked at Michele. "Nothing!"

"Then you will tell me, won't you, Angelo, about the cove?"

"Why do you want to know?"

"Why? Why do you think? I want to keep Herre Nordstrom from going there."

Angelo patted Michele's arm. "Do not worry, my little friend. Herre Nordstrom will never go to the cove."

"How do you know? How can you be so sure?"

"Sure? Of course I am sure. Use your head, Michele. How could he possibly get there? Does he have a small boat?"

"No."

"Then, you see, there is nothing to worry about."

"That is what you think. He is going to get one."

"Where?"

"In Naples."

"Naples?"

"Yes. He is very wealthy. Money, expense—they mean nothing to him."

"All right, all right. He goes to Naples and gets a boat. But once he gets back here, will he be able to row it in these waters?"

"I doubt it."

"Good. Now do you see? You have nothing to worry about. With the first high wave he will come splashing back to shore."

Michele nodded. "I thought that too, but Lord Derby says something else. He says Herre Nordstrom has spent all his life reading and studying. He says he is so smart he doesn't have enough sense to be afraid."

"Ah!" Angelo shook his head. "That is different. You should have told me right away."

"Told you what, Angelo?"

"That he is a smart fool. That makes everything different. A smart fool—there is nothing in the world as dangerous as a smart fool. He will try anything."

"Angelo?"

"Yes, Michele?"

"What are we going to do?"

"We? Why we? I am a simple fisherman, minding my own business. Why we?"

"All right then, I. What am I going to do?"

"Go back to the inn."

"Why?"

"Why? Why? So I can think!"

"Oh, Angelo, do you think you will be able to think of a way to keep him from going?"

"I think only one thing. I think I cannot think with so much talking going on around here."

"Oh, Angelo, you're wonderful! I knew you'd help me. I knew."

"I make no promises. Now go."

"Thank you, Angelo. Thank—"

"For what?"

"For thinking."

"I haven't started yet."

"But you will. You said you would."

"With you around? Never!"

"But I won't be here. I'm going."

"When?"

"Now."

"I don't believe it."

"I'll show you." Michele stood up and the boat tipped forward.

Angelo groaned. "You'll drown us both first."

"You?" Michele laughed. "It would be easier to drown a cork."

"See, I told you."

"What?"

"You're never going."

"I am."

"You're not. You're still here talking."

Michele jumped to the beach. "Good-by, Angelo. I hope—"

"No hopes. No promises. Remember."

"All right, Angelo. Good-by. Good luck."

"All right, Michele. Good-by." He gave a loud groan. "Good riddance!"

Back at the inn Michele tiptoed carefully up the stairs, then turned around and stomped down, as if he had just come out of his room. He could tell by the kitchen noises that he was late, and he was afraid of the questions that might be waiting for him. Opening the door, he rubbed his eyes, yawned, stretched, and tried to look sleepy.

"*Tutto! Tutti!* Tra-la-la-la. Tra-la-la-la." The song came from the far end of the kitchen and filled the room. "*Tutto! Tutti!* Tra-la-la-la."

Michele stopped in the middle of a yawn and smiled. He was in luck. His mother was singing her soft-boiled-egg song and had ears for nothing else. The song had three stanzas and three choruses, and when it was finished the eggs would be done. It was an old recipe. But the song had to be perfect.

Signora Pagano demanded complete silence while she was singing. One interruption, one note held too long, and the eggs would be ruined.

Michele hurried to his mother's side and hid behind her song. Here he was safe. No one, not even his father, would dare to ask questions until the final verse was finished. By that time even his lateness might be forgotten.

Finally the song and the eggs were finished. Signora Pagano gave a great sigh and lifted the eggs from the boiling water. Signor Pagano, who had been walking about on tip-toe, gratefully lowered his heels. Michele, the safety of the song gone, pretended to be counting the breakfast plates.

"Michele!"

"Yes, Papa?"

"Michele, come here."

Michele walked slowly across the room. "Yes, Papa?"

"Michele," Signor Pagano's voice was scarcely a whisper, "Michele, our troubles are over."

"Over, Papa?"

"Yes."

"Why?"

"Look!" Signor Pagano pointed toward the fireplace. "Look! What do you see?"

"I see a chair with Herre Nordstrom in it."

Signor Pagano nodded. "And what is our dear friend Herre Nordstrom doing?"

"He is reading a book."

Signor Pagano rubbed his hands together. "Fine. Fine.

And does our friend look as if he is going out, like Signor Cristoforo Columbo, to make wonderful discoveries and startle the world?"

Michele laughed. "No, he does not."

"Listen, Michele. Herre Nordstrom came downstairs this morning, had his breakfast, sat down in that chair over there, and has had his nose in a book ever since. Already he has forgotten all about the cove."

Signora Pagano, passing triumphantly with her eggs, nodded. "You are right, Papa. He has forgotten all about it. The poor boy! He got excited last night and lost his head. We must not blame him. Scholars! They are all alike. They know a lot of fine words, and they like to use them. But say 'boo' to them and they scurry back to their books like scared rabbits."

For a few minutes Michele felt relieved and happy. Then he remembered Angelo. As always, Angelo was right. Herre Nordstrom wasn't going. It had all been a lot of talk—nothing more. Angelo was right, and he, Michele, was wrong. And now there was Angelo, thinking, thinking, thinking. Michele shivered. He had learned from experience that when Angelo started thinking, things began to happen. Who knew where Angelo's thinking might take him? Who knew what he might be doing this very minute?

"Please, Papa, please, could I run down and see Angelo for a few minutes?"

"Angelo? Why Angelo at this time of the morning?"

"Please, Papa."

"Why do you want to see him?"

"To talk to him."

"About what?"

"Nothing. I just—"

"Well, next week, perhaps, when we aren't so busy."

"Next week?"

"One can talk about nothing just as well next week as this morning, and Angelo will still be there. He will not fly away. Lord Derby is waiting for his breakfast."

Michele spent the day in a daze. He would look at Herre Nordstrom, still in his corner, and feel wonderfully happy. Then he would think of Angelo and his thinking, and feel unbelievably miserable. No one knew what Angelo might do once he got started. Given a good excuse, he would try anything.

Michele was willing to try anything in order to get to Angelo. If he could find some excuse for going to the village, it would take only a few minutes more to reach Angelo's house. And if he ran all the way, no one would ever know the difference.

Didn't his mother need some fish from the market?

No.

Didn't they need wood?

No.

Didn't they—

No.

Nothing worked.

The day passed slowly—breakfast, lunch, dinner. Finally

the last dish was washed and put away. Michele closed the last cabinet door with a thankful bang. He had one more plan left. He would pretend he was sleepy, go to his room, crawl out through the window, climb down the chimney stones, and, with a little moonlight and a lot of luck, he could get to Angelo's house and back without too much trouble.

"Ah!" Signor Pagano came into the kitchen and began to take down the wineglasses. "Come, Mamma, Michele, we are going to have a little celebration." he leaned over and whispered to the two of them, "Herre Nordstrom has not mentioned the cove all day. What better reason could one have to celebrate?"

He put the glasses and an old bottle of wine on a tray and carried them over to the fireplace. Signora Pagano, wiping her hands on her apron, walked behind him. Michele, still deep in his plan, absent-mindedly followed them.

Lord Derby, looking up, saw the little procession come into the room and raised his eyebrows. "Eh? What is this, Signor Pagano?"

Signor Pagano beamed. "A celebration."

"A celebration?" Monsieur Jacques looked up too, and so did Herre Nordstrom. "A celebration? Why?"

Why? Signor Pagano stopped. Why, indeed? What could he say? He dared not mention the real reason. If he complimented Herre Nordstrom on forgetting the cove he might only remind him again.

"Why?" Signor Pagano passed the glasses around slowly, trying to think. "Why?" Then he began to smile. "Why, indeed?" he said, taking a deep breath. "Why celebrate to-day? Today is nothing. Today is a simple, common day. A plain Tuesday of a day. Nothing ever happened today. No important person was born, no battle was fought, no war was won. It is not a saint's day or a holiday. So I suppose we cannot celebrate? Bah!" Signor Pagano cleared his throat and took another deep breath. "Signori, let us take the days of the year. They pass by us in a long procession. Then suddenly a big, important day comes along, its head held high. And it says to everyone, 'Today you may celebrate!' But perhaps I do not feel like celebrating that day. Perhaps, instead, I feel like making faces at everyone or crawling under the bed. Who knows? But today I feel gay. Wonderful! Today, for me—inside of me—it is a holiday. A Pagano day. Signori, I propose a toast. A toast to the—"

"To the cove!" Herre Nordstrom shouted the words. His glass was held higher than any of the others. "A toast to the cove, Signor Pagano. And a toast to the truth."

Signor Pagano lowered his wineglass and put it on the table. "I cannot drink to that, Herre Nordstrom. We hoped, we prayed, you had forgotten all about it."

"Forgotten about the cove? How could I? Why should I?"

"*Mamma mia!* For your own good we hoped! For—"

Outside the wind blew more furiously than ever. Shutters banged against the windows, branches scraped and scratched against the house, something banged against the door. Something or someone. For a minute everyone was silent. Then it came again: three hard, loud knocks.

"Michele, the door."

But Michele was already there. He lifted the latch and pulled it open. "Angelo!"

"Good evening, Michele."

"Angelo—"

Angelo glanced around the room, then looked at Signora Pagano questioningly. "I am very dusty, Signora." He began to brush his coat with his hands. "The sirocco—it grows worse every minute."

Signora Pagano walked toward him, looking a little embarrassed. "Angelo, I have never thanked you for those fish you sent one day, not so very long ago. They saved—"

"Ho!" Angelo laughed. "They were nothing. Had I not sent them to you I would have thrown them back into the ocean."

"Angelo!" Signora Pagano put her hands on her hips and sighed. "Angelo, can't you ever tell the truth? Ever? You know they were wonderful fish. I think they were the best I ever tasted."

"That was not the fish, Signora Pagano, but the way you cooked them. I have heard it said that you could talk a stone into tasting sweet and juicy."

"Humph!" Signora Pagano tried hard not to smile. "Humph! I would be much more pleased, I assure you, if I could talk some people into telling the truth."

"Angelo?" Lord Derby left his place by the fire and walked toward the door. "Are you the fellow we saw on the beach the day we arrived?"

Angelo smiled. "There is only one Angelo, and I am he."

"Then I must thank you too," Lord Derby went on. "I must thank you for sending us to this place. It is, as you said, quiet and peaceful." He looked at Herre Nordstrom out of the corners of his eyes. "At least it was quiet and peaceful until last night. Since then—"

Angelo nodded. "I know. That is why I am here."

"You?" Signor Pagano hurried toward them. "You, Angelo? How do you know about all this?"

Michele looked from Angelo to his father. "I—I told him, Papa."

"You told him? When?"

"This morning, before you were awake."

"Before! Michele, you shouldn't have."

"I had to do something, Papa. I couldn't just sit here and let Herre Nordstrom go off!"

Signor Pagano looked first at Michele and then at Angelo. "And I suppose Angelo is going to stop him?"

"Of course, of course." Signora Pagano gave a little laugh. "Have you forgotten, Papa? Angelo can do anything."

Signor Pagano paid no attention. He looked only at Michele. "Michele, you shouldn't have—"

"It is all right." Angelo patted Signor Pagano on the back. "It is all right. You know that I'm your friend. I will say nothing to anyone. And perhaps I can help."

"How?"

Angelo looked across the room. "Herre Nordstrom?"

"Yes, Angelo?"

"Herre Nordstrom, I have come here tonight to tell you about the cove."

"If you are trying to frighten me, Angelo, it is no use."

"I am not trying to frighten you, I am trying to warn you."

"I thought no one would talk about the cove. Why are *you* willing to talk about it?"

"Because I think my friends are in trouble and I want to help them. Because I hate to see a young fellow like you throw away his life."

Herre Nordstrom stood up and made himself as tall as possible. "Why is everyone so sure I am going to throw away my life?"

"Can you swim, Herre Nordstrom?"

"No."

"Can you row a boat?"

"A little."

"A little!" Angelo put his hands to his head and rocked back and forth. "A little! *Mamma mia!* He says he can row a little—and *he* is going to the cove."

"Why not?" Herre Nordstrom's face began to turn red. "Well, why not? The waters around there look calm enough."

Angelo waved his hands above his head. "Only a *stupido* would say such a thing. It is the rocks you cannot see, Herre Nordstrom, that punch holes in your boat."

"You are just trying to frighten me." Herre Nordstrom's eyes flashed. "You do not want me to go, so you try to frighten me."

Angelo sat down on a low stool close to the fireplace. "Come, come." He waved his hands. "Come, sit down all of you. Sit down and I will tell you about the cove. The cove!" He shrugged his shoulders. "It is a long story and it has no beginning."

Monsieur Jacques laughed. "Last night Signor Pagano said it was a long story without an end."

"That's right." Angelo nodded. "It has no end and no beginning. As far back as anyone can remember, the people of Capri have feared the cove. No one knows when it started." He looked hard at Herre Nordstrom. "No one knows how it will end. But first of all you must know one thing: at the end of the cove there is a cave."

Herre Nordstrom leaned forward. "How do you know?"

"I know. Everyone knows. It can be seen at certain times. When the tide is low and the sun is just right, you can see the mouth very plainly. At high tide it disappears altogether."

Herre Nordstrom leaned back in his chair. "All right," he said, "there is a cave. What is so terrible about a cave?"

Angelo looked down his nose at him. "Would you like to get caught in one when the tide came in?"

"Of course not." Herre Nordstrom gave a short laugh. "But why should one get caught? The tide does not rise and fall so quickly. One could easily get in and out again."

"One could easily get in, Herre Nordstrom."

"And why not out again?"

"That would depend on what you find inside the cave."

"Find? What could I find?"

"Many things, perhaps."

"What things?"

"There are many stories."

"I am all ears, Angelo."

"Some say there are man-eating fish in the cave."

"Man-eating fish? Do you believe that?"

Angelo raised his eyebrows. "I know there *are* man-eating fish, Herre Nordstrom."

"In these waters?"

Angelo shrugged. "Strange fish have been found in strange places, Herre Nordstrom. Who can tell a fish where to live?"

"All right. Man-eating fish! What other stories do they tell, Angelo?"

"They say the mouth of the cave opens and closes at certain times."

Herre Nordstrom laughed. "But that is impossible. Ridiculous!"

"Is it? If someone were there to open and close it, would it be impossible, Herre Nordstrom?"

"Someone? What do you mean?"

"I mean this. As long as anyone can remember, Capri has been a favorite spot for pirates. They have been driven away, time and again, but they always return. Sometimes for ten years, fifteen years, no one will hear of them. Then suddenly—"

Herre Nordstrom looked at him sharply. "You think pirates might be using the cave in the cove?"

Angelo shrugged. "Many pirates have used many caves, Herre Nordstrom. Like the fish, no one can tell them where to live."

"Man-eating fish. Pirates." Herre Nordstrom seemed to be weighing the words. "All right, Angelo. What other stories?"

"The next are not stories. They are facts."

"Good. I like facts."

"Then you will delight in these, Herre Nordstrom, and you can discover them for yourself. For the first one you will need your ears. Take your ears, Herre Nordstrom, and a boat, and row out toward the cove. When you come within sight of it, stop. Pull in your oars and perk up your ears. Then listen. I do not know what you will hear, but I am sure you will hear something. I have heard deep roars and angry hissing. I have heard moaning and groaning. I have heard a strange rattling sound, as if chains were being dragged across the rocks. I have heard a heavy grating noise, as if a huge door were being closed." Angelo stopped for a minute and then went on. "For the second fact, Herre Nordstrom, you will need your eyes. Take them for a walk some day and look around you on Capri. You will see a great deal of volcanic rock. You will see Vesuvius over there in the Bay of Naples. She is asleep now, but she does not always sleep. Sometimes she wakes with a roar, sending out clouds of steam, columns of dust, and streams of lava. Look at our next-door neighbor, the island of Ischia. She has had so many earthquakes no one bothers to count them any more. When the earth moves, Herre Nordstrom, strange things happen. Who knows what has happened, or might be happening, inside that cave?"

Herre Nordstrom nodded his head slowly. "You are right, Angelo, but it is hard to believe that in all these years no one has had the courage, or the curiosity, to find out the truth about this place."

"Two people did."

"Two people? Who?"

"Two priests. Two priests were brave enough. They did not believe the old superstitions and were determined to find out the truth. They swam out to the cove one morning—two young priests, strong and healthy. But late that afternoon a fisherman found them on the beach, more dead than alive. He carried them to his cottage and did what he could to make them comfortable. In the middle of the night one priest cried out, 'The water—it was freezing, like liquid ice.' And the other priest answered, 'The cave—it was on fire with blue flames.' A few minutes later they were both dead.

"In memory of these two priests," Angelo went on, "the people of Capri made a solemn pledge never to mention the cove again." He spread his hands before him. "So you see what you have. You have an old superstition, a solemn pledge to the Church, and a great fear of the mysterious cave. Weave these together and you have something very strong."

Herre Nordstrom nodded. "I understand how the people feel, Angelo, but don't you see?—I don't feel that way myself. Take what the priests said, for instance. It doesn't make sense."

Angelo looked up quickly. "You don't believe that the water could be liquid ice, Herre Nordstrom?"

"Yes, yes, of course. Naturally the water could be very cold. But blue flames! Flames are red and yellow. Who ever heard of blue flames?"

Angelo smiled. "Have you ever seen a fire, Herre Nordstrom?"

"Of course I have seen a fire. What kind of question is that? I am looking at a fire right now."

"You are looking at a fire, Herre Nordstrom, but have you ever seen one? To look and to see are two different things. Anyone with eyes can look. Few people really see. Look at the flames, Herre Nordstrom. They are yellow around the edges, then red, but in the very center, down toward the bottom, you will see, if you really look, that they are blue. That is the hot part of the flame, Herre Nordstrom. And flames that are all blue"—Angelo shook his head—"they would be hot indeed. Hotter than anything you can imagine —or I can imagine."

Herre Nordstrom spoke very slowly. "Angelo," he said, "I'm going to that cave."

Angelo looked just as determined as Herre Nordstrom.

He too spoke very slowly. "Herre Nordstrom, I came here tonight for two reasons: first, I came to persuade you not to go."

"No one can do that, Angelo."

"And second," Angelo went on as if he had not been interrupted, "and second, I came to tell you that if you do go" —he waited a second or two and then went on—"if you do go, Herre Nordstrom, I am going with you."

"What!" Signor Pagano jumped from his chair. "Angelo, you cannot go."

"Why not?"

"Why should you?"

"If I go, Herre Nordstrom has at least a chance to get to the cave. Of course I cannot promise that he will get back."

"Bah! Why should you risk your life to save a—a—" He glared at Herre Nordstrom.

"Well"—Angelo looked at Signora Pagano out of the corners of his eyes and smiled—"well, I guess I've told some pretty big stories in my life." He beat his chest with his fists and grinned. "I, the great Angelo, am afraid of nothing. Now I have a chance to show that I'm as good as I think I am." He winked at Michele. "Maybe even better than I think I am, eh, Michele?"

"If anyone goes, I should go," Signor Pagano shouted. "Herre Nordstrom is my guest. He is my responsibility."

"I should go." Monsieur Jacques walked back and forth across the room. "If anyone goes, I should go. I started all this. It was my idea."

"If you go, I go." Lord Derby blew on his mustaches and cleared his throat.

"Mamma, if Papa goes, I'm going too."

"No, Michele."

"Yes, Mamma, you have to let me. Papa will need me. You know he can't swim a stroke and—"

"Hush! Hush! No one is going."

"They are! They are! Everyone is going."

It seemed that Michele was right. Heads nodded, arms waved, shoulders shrugged. Eyebrows and mustaches rose and fell. Backs straightened, chins went up, chests expanded. Voices rose higher and higher.

Finally Monsieur Jacques' voice rose above the others. "All right, everyone! It's settled. We're all going. We'll leave tomorrow."

"Tomorrow!" Angelo's voice sounded like thunder. "Tomorrow? Have you gone mad? Next month, perhaps, if we are lucky."

"Next month?" Everyone stared at Angelo. "That is fantastic! Ridiculous! Insane!"

"Listen." Angelo spoke slowly, and suddenly everyone was quiet. "Listen to me. It is insane to go at all. Everything is against us. But since we are going, we must make it as sane as possible."

"What do you mean?"

"Mean? I mean this. It will take at least a week to see about the boats. They will not be easy to get." Angelo looked at Herre Nordstrom. "We might, you know, have to go all the way to Naples to get them. Next, I must spend at least a week, maybe more, watching the tide, and I will have to do it secretly. Secretly! That must be our watchword, our motto, our pledge to ourselves and to each other. I do not know what we will find in the cave. I *do* know that the waters of the cove are dangerous. But more dangerous than the cave or the cove are the people of Capri. If they find out about our plans they will do anything to stop us. Anything!" Angelo picked up his cap and started toward the door. "Now I tell you good night, Signori. I'm tired."

Suddenly all the excitement was gone. Everyone looked tired and a little bewildered—everyone except Signora Pagano. She smiled to herself. For the men even to think about going to the cave was of course ridiculous. But let them make their plans—they hadn't gone yet. Within a month anything could happen. Anything—or something. Already a little plan was beginning to run through her mind.

VII. "WHAT IS SO DIFFICULT ABOUT AN EGG?"

When Michele came into the kitchen the next morning his father was standing in front of the stove where his mother usually stood.

"Good morning, Papa."

"Good morning, Michele."

"Where is Mamma?"

"Upstairs."

"Upstairs?" If Signor Pagano had said that Signora Pagano had suddenly left for Paris, Michele would not have been more surprised. His mother was never upstairs at this hour of the morning. As long as Michele could remember, every morning, when he came into the kitchen, his mother was standing in front of the stove, cooking breakfast.

"Upstairs?" he repeated. It was a question and an exclamation together. "Where upstairs?"

"In bed."

"In bed?" Michele could not believe his ears. His mother

in bed at this hour of the morning? It was unthinkable. Suddenly he was frightened. "Is she ill?"

"No."

"No? Not ill—and in bed?" This was really unbelievable. "Then why is she in bed?"

"She says she's sleepy."

Sleepy? His mother? The thought that his mother might ever be sleepy had never occurred to Michele. She was always up when he got up in the morning. She was always up when he went to bed at night. Why had she suddenly decided to be sleepy?

Signor Pagano looked at Michele out of the corners of his eyes. "Michele, your mother is in bed because—well, because she says she isn't going to do anything any more. She says she isn't going to cook, or take care of the inn, or—or anything. She says if we can be stubborn about going to the cove, she can be stubborn too."

Michele stared at his father. "But, Papa, if she does that the men will leave!"

"I know, I know. That's what your mother wants them to do. She wants them to leave."

"Wants them to leave? But they are paying us well, and it is winter."

"I know. But your mother says if we all go to the cove we will be ruined. One way or the other, she says, we will be ruined. If we go, and something happens to us—" Signor Pagano spread his hands in front of him and shrugged his shoulders. "And if we go and do get back, Mamma says no one on Capri will ever speak to us again. Either way, Mamma says, we will be ruined."

"What do you think about it?"

Signor Pagano shrugged again. "I do not know, Michele. I only know that I cannot back out now. I have said I will go. And I will go. To tell you the truth, I am as eager as Herre Nordstrom to find out the truth about the cove. It has tormented me for many years. Now, after all this time, to have a chance to go— It is too much. I couldn't give it up."

Michele smiled. Right now, to him, nothing seemed as important as exploring the cove. He was glad his father felt the same way about it. "But what about Mamma?" he asked.

Signor Pagano shook his head. "We can do nothing about Mamma, Michele. You and I, we will have to carry on as best we can."

"Of course, Papa. You've helped Mamma with the cooking. So have I. We'll get along all right."

Signor Pagano nodded. "Cooking—it is nothing. Women make a big fuss about it. It is a game they play with themselves. It makes them feel important. Give anyone a few pots and pans, some food and a little heat, and he can make a meal. Even us. Eh, Michele?"

"Of course, Papa."

"First"—Signor Pagano rubbed his hands together—"first we must fix Lord Derby two soft-boiled eggs. He has them every morning for breakfast."

Two soft-boiled eggs! At the mention of them Michele and his father thought of Signora Pagano's soft-boiled-egg

song, and they began to laugh. Two soft-boiled eggs! Signor
Pagano winked at Michele. He took a small pot, filled it with
water, and dropped in two eggs.

"Papa, I think Mamma has the water boiling before she
puts in the eggs."

"Really?"

"I think so."

"Are you sure?"

"No."

"Well, it is not too important one way or the other. The
eggs, they are not too particular. But if you think it is right
we will let the water boil first." He took the eggs out of the
pot and put them on a table that stood beside the stove.

The table, an old wooden one, had been scraped and
scoured for many years. It was slightly higher in the center,
but only an egg would have noticed the gentle slope. These
eggs, the two of them, noticed it immediately; and while
Signor Pagano was bent over the fire, they rolled slowly down
the incline and fell with a squash onto the floor.

Signor Pagano jumped as if he had been shot in the back.
Then he stared at the eggs. Shells, yolks, and whites quivered
in a messy puddle at his feet.

Michele, wanting to help, stooped down to pick them up.
The shells were picked up quickly, but when he tried to take
up the whites and yolks they ran through his fingers.

"Here." Signor Pagano handed Michele a towel. "Use
this."

Michele took the towel, then looked up at his father. "It's

one of Mamma's best towels," he said. "I don't think she would like us to use it on the floor."

"Mamma! Mamma!" Signor Pagano was losing his patience. "If Mamma wants to protect her towels she should be down here instead of upstairs asleep. Use it. A little dirt won't ruin it forever."

Michele wiped up the eggs and put the towel on the cupboard. Then he got two more eggs out of the basket. By this time the water was boiling briskly.

Michele handed the eggs to his father, who dropped them quickly into the water. Too quickly! The eggs were cold, having been outside all night, and the water was boiling. Instantly the shells broke and the white oozed out, making great curlicues of solid white in the little pot.

This would never do. Signor Pagano took a large spoon, fished them out, and threw them into the garbage. "Two more eggs, Michele."

This time Signor Pagano put the eggs into a spoon and lowered them slowly into the water. Finally they were completely submerged, the shells remained whole, and the water bubbled gently around them.

"Ah!" Signor Pagano rubbed his hands together. "In a few minutes now, Michele, Lord Derby's eggs will be ready. We had a couple of accidents, yes. But accidents will happen to anyone. A soft-boiled egg—what is so difficult about a soft-boiled egg? Now we will show Mamma that one does not have to be a grand opera singer in order to boil a couple of eggs."

Michele took down the plates while Signor Pagano hovered anxiously over the eggs. Then, a few seconds later, they heard Lord Derby coming down the stairs.

"Ah!" Signor Pagano wiped his hands on his apron. "He is just in time, Michele, just in time. The eggs are ready." He lifted them out of the water and struck each of them sharply across the center with a knife. Then he picked one up and held it expectantly over a small bowl. Out came the white and the yolk, but neither looked as if they had been long away from the hen's nest.

"Papa, they aren't done."

"They aren't done." Signor Pagano repeated the words slowly. It was hard to believe, still there they were, like so much water. Signor Pagano took a deep breath. "Two more eggs, Michele."

Once more Signor Pagano lowered the eggs into the boiling water. "Well," he said, laughing good-naturedly, "they take a little longer than I thought. A little longer. Take some fruit in to Lord Derby, Michele, and talk to him for a while. Get his mind off his breakfast. Give me a little time. These eggs will be perfect. You'll see. Perfect."

"Shall I talk about the cove?"

"The cove, the weather, anything. Just give me a chance to cook these eggs."

Michele walked into the dining room. "Good morning, Lord Derby."

"Good morning, Michele."

"A nice day, Lord Derby."

"Is it?" Lord Derby looked out of the window. "I hadn't noticed. I don't feel so well this morning, Michele. I didn't sleep well last night. Too much excitement, I suppose. Maybe I'll feel better after I've had my breakfast. I usually do. I like my breakfast, Michele. Always have. Best meal of the day, I always say. Best meal of the day. And do you want to know something, Michele? I always have two soft-boiled eggs for breakfast. Always have. No matter where I go. Two soft-boiled eggs." Lord Derby leaned back in his chair. "You know that's something to think about, Michele. I'm fifty years old, and as long as I can remember I've had two soft-boiled eggs for breakfast. That's a goodly number of eggs, Michele."

"It is indeed, Lord Derby."

"I wonder how many that would be?"

"I haven't any idea, Lord Derby."

"Well, it's easy enough to figure. Let's see. Fifty times three hundred and sixty-five is—" Lord Derby closed his eyes. "That's eighteen thousand two hundred and fifty, Michele. And two times that—I figure it's about thirty-six thousand five hundred. Well"—he laughed—"I guess I didn't start eating them the day I was born. We'll take off the five hundred just to be fair. That still leaves thirty-six-thousand. That's quite a few eggs, wouldn't you say, Michele?"

"Yes, it is, Lord Derby. It certainly is." Michele thought of his father and the two eggs boiling in the pot. They seemed very small compared with thirty-six thousand, but very important. Somehow he didn't have the confidence in their success that his father seemed to have. He smiled weakly. "I should think you would get tired of so many soft-boiled eggs, Lord Derby. I should think you'd like them cooked some other way for a change. Scrambled, or fried, or —or an omelet."

"Never." Lord Derby's big voice filled the room. "Never, Michele. I'm a creature of habit. Couldn't live without my soft-boiled eggs to start me off in the morning. Why, once when I was hunting in Africa they couldn't find any hen's eggs for me and I had to eat an ostrich egg. Biggest—"

"Michele!" The call from the kitchen was a cry for help. "Michele!"

"Excuse me, Lord Derby." Michele hurried toward the door. "Excuse me, my father—" He was out of the room before he could finish.

"Michele! Look!"

Michele looked. In his father's hand there was a small bowl, and in the bowl were two eggs—two hard-boiled eggs, two eggs like rocks, two eggs with the yolks a little green around the edges.

"Papa!"

Signor Pagano glared at the eggs. Then, appealingly, he looked at Michele. "Michele, I have wasted six eggs already this morning. With these, two it will be eight. Eight eggs, Michele. That is a lot of eggs to waste."

"Yes, Papa."

"Michele, we must eat these eggs, you and I, so they will not be wasted."

"But, Papa, hard-boiled eggs before breakfast?" Michele gulped. He could already feel the dry yolk in his throat.

"I know, Michele. I know. But really we cannot waste them. Six is bad enough. But eight! That is unthinkable. We cannot afford it. We must eat them. Come. It will not be too bad. You take one and I'll take the other."

"But, Papa, couldn't we save them until later—around lunchtime maybe?"

"And let Mamma find them? She would tease me for the rest of my life."

After that Michele could not refuse. So, standing in the middle of the kitchen, he and his father ate the eggs, swallowing them dutifully, like so much medicine.

At last they were down. Signor Pagano wiped his mouth with the end of his apron. He looked at the stove, at the kettle with the boiling water, at the eggs, at Michele.

"Michele, do you happen to know—do you happen to remember—do you—" He looked at Michele a little sheepishly. "Michele, do you happen to remember that soft-boiled-egg song your mother sings?"

The soft-boiled-egg song! Michele remembered how many times he and his father had teased her about it. Now, suddenly, it was of the greatest importance. Everything depended upon it, everything. If he could remember the song the eggs might turn out all right. If the eggs were all right, Lord Derby would be satisfied. If Lord Derby was satisfied, he would stay. If he stayed, the others would stay too. If the others stayed— Michele thought if he could only keep them at the inn this one day his mother would soon relent and come to their rescue. He could not imagine his mother staying away from her kitchen more than a day. The soft-boiled-egg song —everything, even the trip to the cove, hung upon it.

"Tra-la-la-la," he began uncertainly. "Tra-la-la-la . . . I can't rememer it. I just can't."

"Never mind." Signor Pagano shook his head. "It can't be helped. It is what we deserve, you and I, after all our teasing." He looked down at the two eggs he held in his hand. Suddenly he was furious. "Soft-boiled eggs! Who ever heard of such a thing? It is ridiculous! Why should anyone be expected to cook an egg when it is still inside the shell? Can you see it or smell it? No. Can you taste it? No. Can you put a fork into it to see if it is done? No. Who can tell what's going on inside? A minute too short and the egg is raw. A minute too long, and what happens?"

Michele grinned. "A minute too long and one eats hard-boiled eggs before breakfast."

Signor Pagano didn't notice the little joke. He was still talking. "An egg is not supposed to be cooked in the shell, Michele. I am sure of it. Is anything else cooked that way? No. What goes on inside that shell is a dark mystery. One must be gifted with a sixth sense to understand such things. Your mother, Michele, is a very wise woman, with six senses. But I, Michele, have only the usual five. There are other ways to cook eggs, Michele. Delicious ways. I shall scramble some eggs for Lord Derby."

"But, Papa—"

"Don't bother me, Michele. My mind is made up."

"But, Papa, Lord Derby just told me he always has soft-boiled eggs for breakfast. He's had thirty-six thousand—"

Signor Pagano was still angry. Everything and everyone was against him: Michele, Lord Derby, the eggs. "Who does Lord Derby think he is anyway?" he murmured to himself. "Bossing people around, day in and day out. It will do him good to find out he can't always have everything just the way he wants it."

Michele shrugged his shoulder. The scrambled eggs would be a dead give-away. Lord Derby would realize at once that Signora Pagano hadn't cooked his breakfast. How could they expect the guests to stay under the circumstances? It was all over. Lord Derby would pack his things and leave. They would all leave. The trip to the cove would be off. His mother would win. A long, eventless winter stretched before him.

But Signor Pagano was still fighting his egg battle. He could think of nothing else. Recklessly he broke two eggs into a skillet and beat them furiously. "Ah!" He beamed first at Michele and then at the eggs. "This is more like it. A man can tell what's going on. They are beautiful, Michele. Beautiful!"

By this time Herre Nordstrom and Monsieur Jacques had joined Lord Derby at the table, so they were in the dining room when Signor Pagano made his triumphant entrance.

"Ah!" Signor Pagano put the bowl of scrambled eggs in front of Lord Derby. They were a little burned in spots, and uncooked in the center, but Signor Pagano looked at them fondly.

Lord Derby, however, was not so impressed. "I think there has been some mistake," he said. "I always have—"

"A little change, Lord Derby." Signor Pagano beamed. "A little variety. It is good for one."

"But I always—"

"Always is a long time, Lord Derby."

"But I—"

"Try them."

"But—"

"One little bite."

Lord Derby pushed his chair away from the table. "Where is Signora Pagano? She always fixes my eggs just right. Why has she suddenly given me this—this scrambled concoction?"

Tears began to roll down Signor Pagano's cheeks. His struggle with the eggs had unnerved him.

"Lord Derby, you might as well know the truth. It is foolish to try to keep it from you."

"The truth?"

"Yes. You see, Signora Pagano— Well," he hurried on, "you see, my wife doesn't approve of our going to the cove. In fact, she very definitely thinks we should not go to the cove. So—well—" Signor Pagano smiled apologetically. "Well, she says she won't cook for us or take care of the inn unless we give up the whole idea."

"Won't cook?" The three men stared at Signor Pagano.

"That's what she says."

"But if she won't cook for us we will have to leave." Lord Derby looked at the scrambled eggs out of the corner of his eye.

Signor Pagano nodded. "I know."

"Doesn't she care?"

Signor Pagano shook his head.

"You mean she wants us to leave?"

Signor Pagano nodded.

"Why?"

"She says if you leave, no one will go to the cove, and all our troubles will be over."

"Well!" Lord Derby pushed the eggs away from him. "That settles that. I suppose I might as well pack my things."

"Pack your things?" Herre Nordstrom looked up. "Why?"

"To leave, of course."

"Sit down. Sit down. No one is leaving."

"Why not?"

"Are you going to let two eggs scare you away from Capri?"

Lord Derby looked a little embarrassed. He pulled his plate toward him again and took a little bite. They were worse than he thought—much worse. They tasted like a combination of glue and burned rubber. He glared at Herre Nordstrom.

Herre Nordstrom leaned forward and looked at all of

them. "This is serious, I'll admit, but it isn't enough to stop us." He looked at Monsieur Jacques. "I've always heard that Frenchmen are good cooks. Is that true?"

"Well—" Monsieur Jacques hesitated.

"Good." Herre Nordstrom slapped him on the back. "Then that's settled. You'll be the cook. Lord Derby can make the beds—"

"Beds!" Lord Derby sputtered. "Beds?"

"Yes, beds." Herre Nordstrom smiled. "You know, the things you sleep in at night. Sheets, pillows, blankets—beds!"

"But I—"

"You'll learn. Now I," Herre Nordstrom went on, "I'll wash the dishes. Signor Pagano can help Monsieur Jacques with the cooking, and Michele can do the marketing. How's that?"

Everyone looked a little startled. Still, when they thought about it for a few minutes it didn't seem too impossible. Finally, one by one, the faces began to relax. Monsieur Jacques hurried toward the kitchen, demanding an apron. Lord Derby started upstairs to make the beds, but Herre Nordstrom called after him, "Lord Derby, come back and eat your eggs."

"But I—"

"Eat your eggs!"

"But—"

"Your eggs!"

Lord Derby took a small bite on his fork and closed his

eyes. Cold now, they were even worse than before. "I—" He looked beseechingly at Herre Nordstrom.

"Eat your eggs, Lord Derby. You can't make beds on an empty stomach."

"I can't make beds on a full stomach either!"

"Never mind. You'll learn."

They all learned. By the end of the week they had all learned to sleep in Lord Derby's lumpy beds, to eat Monsieur Jacques' impossible cooking, and not to look at Herre Nordstrom's half-washed dishes. They learned, too, to smile sweetly at Signora Pagano when she walked through the inn or sat in the patio. She herself, when the others were out of the way, slipped into the kitchen and fixed herself all kinds of wonderful-smelling food. And this was the hardest of all to bear. They could learn to take Lord Derby's beds, and Monsieur Jacques' cooking, and Herre Nordstrom's dish-washing, but they could not learn to ignore those wonderful smells that came from the kitchen.

For Signor Pagano it was the hardest of all. Finally he could stand it no longer.

"Mamma, won't you come back and cook for us?"

"No!"

"Why not?"

"You know why not."

"Mamma, the men are going to the cove anyway, you know that now. Nothing anyone does or doesn't do is going to stop them."

"Just because they are going, you don't have to go."

"But I can't refuse to go after I said I would go. I can't back out now."

Signora Pagano shrugged her shoulders. "It is bad enough for you to go, bad enough. But to take Michele with you! To take a fourteen-year-old boy with you, when you don't know what might happen to him. To—to—" Signora Pagano began to cry.

"Mamma?"

A muffled "Yes, Papa," came from behind her handkerchief.

"Mamma, listen. I have thought about all this a great deal. I will tell you why I am taking Michele with me."

Signora Pagano began to cry louder. "It will be the end of all of us," she sobbed. "The end of all of us."

"Mamma, listen. You know we are poor. You know that. You know we have nothing to give Michele. Nothing."

"Yes, I know that."

"We have nothing to give him. I cannot afford to send him to school to learn to be a doctor or a priest or a teacher, can I?"

"No."

"And I can't let him travel to all the places he would like to go. I can't do that either."

"No."

"And I can't give him any money to buy a little land, so he could raise a few vegetables for himself, or some olives, perhaps, or some grapes—maybe even a pig. I can't do that either."

"No."

"I can't even let him go away from here, to be a sailor, or to work for someone else in some big city. No, I can't even do that, because we need him here to help us with the inn. We couldn't even let him go across the bay to Naples when Salaro wanted to take him. Even that we couldn't give him. You see, there is nothing we can give him. He has nothing to look forward to but years of hard work here in this old inn. Years and years and years. We are poor, and will always be poor, I suppose, and Michele will be poor after us. Isn't that true, Mamma?"

"Yes."

"So last week I had nothing to give to Michele, but now—now I have something."

"Now you have something?" Signora Pagano looked up. "What do you have now?"

"Now I have a chance to give him an adventure. That is all a poor man can give his son, Mamma, a chance for an adventure. Listen. If we go to the cove and come back, Michele will have had an experience he will never forget. He will tell his children about it, and his grandchildren. It will be something for him to think about when he is working hard at the inn. It will make him proud that he had the courage to go. It will make him feel brave inside, brave and important. That is all I have to give Michele, a bit of adventure. Surely that is not too much. Surely you would not want me to take this one thing away from him."

"But suppose something should happen to him? Suppose he shouldn't come back? Remember the two priests!"

"Mamma, listen. I have figured it all out. There will be five men and Michele. That will mean at least three boats. The cove is very narrow, so the boats will have to enter it one at a time. I promise you that Michele will be in the last boat. If anything happens to the first boat, I will send Michele back."

"But what if there are pirates—and they shoot at you?"

"Michele can swim well under water. They would have a hard time hitting him."

"Will you stay in the third boat with Michele?"

"If it makes you feel better, I'll promise to do that too."

"It will make me feel better."

"Good! Then I promise."

"You will come back if anything happens?"

"Yes. You understand now, don't you, Mamma? You understand why I must go, and why I must let Michele go with me?"

"Yes."

"Then you will come back and cook for us?"

"No!"

"Why not?"

"Because I still don't think you should go. I still think the whole idea is dangerous, ridiculous, insane!"

"Mamma! You said you understood!"

"I do understand, but I still don't think you should go."

"We'll go whether you cook for us or not!"

"All right! All right! Go! Stay! Do whatever you like! But I won't cook for a houseful of imbeciles!"

At that moment Monsiuer Jacques opened the kitchen door and set down a charred kettle that was smoking like a live coal.

"My kettle!" Signora Pagano sprang to her feet. "My kettle! My favorite kettle! Look what he has done to it!" She ran toward the kitchen, waving her hands. "Out of my kitchen! Out! Out! Thief! Robber! Out of my kitchen! My best kettle! My best kettle! Look what you've done to it! Look!"

Monsieur Jacques looked. It was, indeed, ruined. "I'm sorry Signora Pagano. I'm sorry."

"Sorry! Being sorry will not give me back my kettle."

"I know Signora Pagano. I know. It is too bad. But listen. In France they make wonderful kettles. When I get back there I will send you a new one, the best I can find."

"A *new* kettle! Humph!"

"What is wrong with a new kettle?"

"Wrong? Everything is wrong with a new kettle."

"Signora Pagano, you don't know what you're saying. You're excited, upset. Here I am offering you a new kettle in place of an old one, and you turn up your nose."

"Of course I turn up my nose, and with good reason. A new kettle is like a new cook, Monsieur Jacques: it doesn't know a thing about cooking."

"Doesn't know—" Monsieur Jacques stopped and stared. Was the woman out of her mind?

Signora Pagano looked at the smoldering kettle on the doorstep and shook her head. "Such a good kettle. Such a joy. Such a comfort. The things it has cooked in its day."

"But Signora Pagano, a new kettle—"

"A new kettle! A new kettle!" Signora Pagano stamped her foot. "Is that all you can think about? Listen, Monsieur Jacques, a new kettle has to learn how to cook, just as a person has to learn how to cook. A new kettle is green, stupid, foolish, unreliable. Things stick to it. It has an odd taste. It cooks too fast or too slowly. It is this way and that way— one can never be sure. It takes a year, sometimes two, to break in a kettle. Let me tell you this, Monsieur Jacques: the second stew cooked in a kettle is better than the first one. The tenth stew is better than the fifth. The two-hundredth stew is better than the hundredth. And when a kettle has cooked a thousand stews—ah! then it is just getting started. Why? Because a kettle has to learn how to cook. Remember that."

"A kettle has to learn how to cook?" Monsieur Jacques shook his head. The woman was impossible. "What do you mean? This kettle was old, the handle was broken, the—"

"One does not cook the stew on the handle, Monsieur. Remember that too. A broken handle! La-la-la. What difference does that make? Would you fire a cook who had gray hair and wrinkles in her face?"

"Well, no, I guess not."

"You guess not! You are a fool, Monsieur. That old kettle knows more about cooking than you'll ever know. Now, out of my kitchen before you ruin something else. Out! Out! Out!"

"Then you will come back and cook for us, Signora Pagano?"

"I will come back and cook, yes. But just to protect my kettles. Understand that. I still think you are all insane, going off to the cove like a bunch of *stupidos*. The cove! Bah! Oh, my poor kettle, my poor kettle! Imbecile!"

VIII. "EIGHT DAYS!"

They didn't see Angelo for a week. Another week passed, and still no Angelo. Herre Nordstrom, Monsieur Jacques, and Lord Derby became very impatient. Even Michele began to wonder what had happened to his friend.

With each passing day, however, Signora Pagano became more and more cheerful, her meals more and more wonderful. She sang and laughed; she talked to the food. It was like old times.

Finally, when fifteen days had passed and Angelo still did not appear, Signora Pagano looked particularly jubilant.

"Michele," she said. "That Angelo, Michele, he is no fool."

Michele looked surprised. "But, Mamma, I thought you didn't like Angelo."

"Did I say that I like him? I only said he was no fool. Do I have to go around liking everyone who is not a fool?"

Michele waited. He knew his mother was leading up to something.

"Yes"—Signora Pagano nodded her head—"Angelo is

no fool. He can be smart when it is smart to be smart. He talked big in front of Herre Nordstrom, in front of everyone: 'I, Angelo, will take you to the cove.' But alone again he realized his foolishness. It is easy to be brave in front of a lot of people. It is much more difficult to be brave alone. So what does Angelo do? He disappears. Without Angelo it will be impossible for the men to go to the cove. They all know that now. Angelo came one night and said, 'I, Angelo, will take you to the cove. I will arrange everything. I will get the boats. I will watch the tides. I will do everything that has to be done.' And the men believe him. They sit back and relax. They wait and they wait and they wait. But no Angelo. No Angelo, no cove. They are helpless without him. Can they get boats? No. Do they know about the tides? No. Do they know anything? No. So they wait and wait for Angelo. Now they are tired of waiting. Even the desire to go to the cove is not so great any more. They are bored and impatient. They are disgusted with Angelo, with themselves, with the inn, with Capri. Soon, the saints be praised, they will be tired of waiting and leave Capri. Then Angelo will come back again. Everything will be as it was before. I tell you, he is no fool, that Angelo. To disappear, to vanish: how wise, how wonderfully wise. Angelo has fixed everything for us. Soon all our troubles will be over. Yes, I am sure of it. Angelo has gone away."

Michele started at his mother. "Angelo gone away? Where could he go?"

"Go? Where couldn't he go? He could go anywhere,

that Angelo. Who is to tell him where to go or where not
to go? There is only one place I am sure he could not go."

"Where?"

"To heaven!" Signora Pagano smiled. Today she was almost ready to let Angelo into heaven, but not quite. Perhaps when the men had really gone—she would see. Certainly she was feeling more and more kindly toward Angelo
all the time. To go away—that was very smart, very clever;
a wonderful way to solve their problems. He was no fool,
that Angelo. Signora Pagano nodded her head. "Yes,
Michele, I am sure of it. Angelo has gone away."

Michele's eyes flashed. "I don't believe it, Mamma.
Angelo would not run away like a coward."

"Who said he was a coward? Sometimes it takes a brave
man to run away."

" 'Sometimes it takes a brave man to run away,' " Michele repeated the words slowly to himself. Was it true? Had
Angelo really gone? Michele knew that Angelo would do
anything to help his friends. He would do anything—even
act like a coward—if he thought it would help. Was his
mother right? Had Angelo gone away in order to keep all
of them from going to the cove? Michele shrugged his
shoulders. Who could tell what Angelo was thinking beneath his gay words? Had his promise to take them been
nothing but a plot—a plot to put them off until, as his
mother said, the men grew tired of waiting for him and went
away?

Signora Pagano beamed. "I have a wonderful idea,

Michele, a wonderful idea. Soon the men will leave. Every day they grow more and more impatient. And, once they have gone, Angelo will come back. Then we will have a celebration, Michele. We will have a grand dinner. We will have a grand dinner for Angelo. What shall we have?"

For the first time in his life Michele was not interested in food. "I don't know, Mamma," he answered dully. "I don't know."

"Fish?" Signora Pagano looked thoughtful, thinking of her best recipes. "No, not fish. One does not have fish as a special treat for a fisherman. Chicken perhaps. Roast chicken. Does Angelo like chicken?"

"Yes, very much!" The answer came from the end of the room.

Michele and his mother looked toward the doorway.

"Angelo!" Michele was delighted. Signora Pagano was furious. "Angelo!"

Michele hurried toward him. "Angelo, where have you been?"

"Been? I've been busy. What do you think? The boy asks me where I've been! I've been getting boats, studying tides, making plans. Where have I been? Where do you think I have been?"

"No place. Only—"

"Only what?"

Angelo's deep voice had filled the inn. Immediately everyone came running: Herre Nordstrom, Lord Derby, Monsieur Jacques, Signor Pagano. "Angelo! Angelo! Angelo!" They crowded around him. They asked him a thousand questions.

Only Michele remained silent. He knew Angelo too well. He knew Angelo could not be hurried.

Angelo sat down in a big chair in front of the fireplace. He looked very serious. "I have three fishing boats," he said, "my own and two others. If anything happens to them, I am responsible."

"Don't worry about that." Herre Nordstrom made a grand gesture with his hand. "I will pay if something happens to them."

"And if something happens to you?"

The words seemed to hang in the air. Everyone was silent. The words filled the room, filled the minds of the men, of Michele, of Signora Pagano. There was no room for any other thoughts.

Finally Herre Nordstrom stood up, took his wallet out of his pocket, and handed some money to Signora Pagano.

"Here," he said. "If I do not come back, give this money to the two fishermen."

Signora Pagano put her hands behind her. "I will not touch the money," she said. "It is wrong. The whole thing is wrong. I will have nothing to do with it."

Herre Nordstrom walked over to the mantel and picked up a small jar. "See," he said, "I am putting the money in here. Surely if I do not come back you will see that the fishermen get it?"

Signora Pagano would not look at Herre Nordstrom. She stared straight ahead at the other end of the room. "If you do not come back," she said slowly, "I will tell the fishermen that the money is here. They can come and get it. But I will not touch it. I will not touch it. You think your money can buy anything—anything!" And she began to cry.

Signor Pagano tried to change the subject. He looked at Angelo. "Tell us, Angelo, how did you get the other two boats?"

"How? I will tell you how. I have two brothers, Giovanni and Antonio. They promised to lend me their boats some Sunday when they're not going fishing."

"What did you tell them, Angelo?"

Angelo shrugged his shoulders. "I did not have to tell them much. Everyone on Capri knows how it is with the tourists. They must be treated like infants—like *bambinos*. If they want the moon, someone must climb up a ladder at night and get it for them. If it rains, someone must turn it off. If the ocean is too cold, we are expected to heat it. A shield must be made for the sun if it shines too brightly. When a tourist buys a ticket he thinks he also buys a piece of heaven. Is it not so, Signor Pagano?"

Signor Pagano looked at his three guests out of the corner of his eye, then quickly nodded his head at Angelo, hoping no one else noticed.

"So," Angelo went on, "I did not have to tell my brothers too much. They were quick to understand. I told them you were having your troubles, Signor Pagano. I told them your three guests wanted to be taken on a little trip in some fishing boats. 'You know how it is,' I said to my two brothers, 'the

tourists, they are a bit queer, not quite right in the head—
they get crazy ideas.' "

"La-la-la." Signora Pagano's voice carried across the room.
"At last Angelo has told the truth about something. This
is a day to remember! 'Not quite right in the head'! 'Crazy
ideas'! It is the truth, Angelo. You are smarter than I
thought."

Lord Derby, however, was not so pleased. "Well!" he said.
"Well! Was that necessary, Angelo? I'm not sure I like all
this. To be called 'queer, not quite right in the head'—that
is going too far, much too far."

"Had I told them the real truth," Angelo answered, "they
would not have thought you queer. They would have thought
you insane. Would you have liked that better?"

"All right, all right." Lord Derby blew on his mustaches.
"Let us forget about it. What has been said, has been said.
What has been done, has been done. The important thing
now is to go to the cove and be finished with it. When do we
go, Angelo?"

"At noon, a week from Sunday."

"At noon? On Sunday?" Everyone looked startled. Even
Michele could not keep silent. "In the middle of the day?
When everyone can see us, Angelo?"

Angelo smiled. "The safest place for a fly is on top of the
fly swatter. The safest place for a secret is out in the open. If
we sneaked down to the boats early in the morning someone
would be sure to see us. If someone saw us he would wonder
what we were doing—and you can be sure he would wonder

out loud. Then buzz, buzz, buzz. In five minutes the whole town would know about it. In ten minutes every man, woman, and child would be down at the harbor to look at us. Every move we made would be watched. A thousand questions would be asked.

"But," Angelo went on, "if we all go down to the boats in the middle of the day, if we talk and laugh and make a big commotion, who will notice us? Who will be interested? Who will care? Who will pay any attention to us?" He looked at Signora Pagano. "If you will lend us your lunch basket, I think we can hide our secret in it. Carrying the basket, we will be six *stupidos* off for the day—nothing more."

Signora Pagano nodded. "All right, Angelo, I will lend you my basket—and I will fill it for you too. Surely you would not want to carry an empty basket?"

Angelo smiled. "You are right, Signora Pagano. Our secret would rattle around in an empty basket. It would be sure to attract attention."

"No." Signora Pagano shook her head. "The basket, it cannot be empty. That would never do. I will fill it for you, Angelo. I will fill it full of rocks."

Angelo stood up and made a deep bow. "If you fix the rocks, Signora Pagano, they will be delicious I'm sure. And just think, you have eight days to cook them!"

Eight days! Suddenly Michele felt very queer. Eight days! In eight days his life was going to be different. No matter what they found or didn't find in the cove, he knew that in some way his life on Capri would never be quite the same

again. Was his mother right? Was it insane to go? Was it
ridiculous to give up their safe, pleasant life for this strange,
doubtful adventure? He looked around the room. Of the six
who were going, how many would still be alive eight days
from now? Would they be shot down, drowned, frozen to
death, eaten alive, frightened, ill? Would they live to tell
what had happened? Eight days!

"Eight days!" Angelo's voice filled the room. "Just eight
days, Signori. That is not much time. There is a great deal to
do. Good day, Signori." And Angelo went out.

IX. "I DIDN'T SAY NO"

Eight days! Michele didn't know whether they went slowly or quickly. The days themselves seemed to drag by, hour after hour; still, surprisingly soon, it was Saturday again. Saturday—and tomorrow would be Sunday. Tomorrow! The word had a special sound. Michele felt as if he had been chasing tomorrows all his life, and now he was about to catch one.

Then, just before he was ready to go to bed Saturday night, Pietro came by. They talked for a while, and then, as Pietro was leaving he called back over his shoulder, "See you tomorrow, Michele."

"Oh!" Michele stared at him. He had forgotten about Pietro. He and Pietro were always together on Sunday. As long as Michele could remember, he and Pietro had done something together on Sunday afternoon. But tomorrow! Michele stared at Pietro as if he were looking at a ghost.

"Michele, what's the matter?"

"Nothing, Pietro. Only—only—Pietro, I won't be able to meet you tomorrow."

"Won't be able to meet me? Why not?"

"I—I just can't."

"Do you have to work?" Pietro came back a few steps and stood close to Michele. "If you have to work, I'll come and help you. Then when we're finished we can—"

"No, I don't have to work, Pietro."

"Then why?" Pietro looked puzzled. He and Michele always told each other everything. Why was Michele acting so queerly?

"Pietro," said Michele. "Pietro, I can't meet you tomorrow. I just can't. And I can't tell you why either. It's a secret. It's a secret I promised not to tell anyone." Michele made a great circle in the dirt with his toe. He didn't want to look at Pietro. He didn't want to see in Pietro's eyes all the things he was thinking.

"Can't tell me?" Pietro shook his head. "You can't tell *me*, Michele? But we always tell each other everything. You know you can trust me. You know that, Michele."

"Oh, I know. I know, Pietro. If it were up to me I'd tell you in a minute. But you see—you see I promised not to tell *anyone!* Not anyone, Pietro. I promised on my honor. You do understand, don't you Pietro?"

Pietro stared at Michele. He didn't understand, that was clear. He and Michele had always shared everything. What was this secret that had come between them? Their life on Capri was so simple. They worked and they ate and they slept. What could Michele do—what could he know—that he could not tell to his best friend?

They stood for a few minutes, staring at the ground. Michele made more circles, Pietro made squares. They had nothing to say to each other.

Finally Pietro turned and started down the hill. "Well, good night, Michele."

"Good night, Pietro."

"I'll see you to—" The words came before Pietro could stop them. "Good night, Michele."

Michele turned and walked back into the inn. He had never been so miserable in all his life. He thought of all the things he and Pietro had done together. "And Pietro would not go to Naples because I couldn't go. Pietro wouldn't go to Naples because I couldn't go." The words repeated themselves over and over. What greater test of friendship could anyone give? And now he, Michele, had shut Pietro out. It was the cove that had come between them. Michele shuddered. Was it really bad luck, as everyone said? Was the cove beginning, already, to cast its evil spell upon him? Michele knew that he and Pietro would always be friends; but somehow, after tonight, their friendship would never be quite the same again. To lose a real friend! Was the cove worth it?

Michele went to bed but he couldn't sleep. He thought of the two priests. He thought of his mother, worrying about them. He thought of the three guests, of his father, of himself. How many of the six who were going to the cove would be sleeping in their beds tomorrow night?

But most of all Michele thought of Pietro. To lose a real

friend! Was the cove worth it? Was any adventure worth it?

Then Michele had an idea. If only Pietro could go with them! If he could tell the secret to Pietro, and he could go with them, then everything would be all right. The two priests, the danger, the evil powers of the cove suddenly seemed unimportant again. If only Pietro could go, everything would be all right.

Michele got out of bed and looked at the sky. The stars were still there, but they were growing fainter. Michele looked eagerly toward the east. As soon as the sun was up he would go and talk to Angelo.

When Michele awoke the sun was high in the sky. He jumped out of bed, dressed quickly, and ran down the stairs to the kitchen. Breakfast was over! The kitchen and the dining room were deserted.

This was a piece of good luck. He could run down to see Angelo, and no one would know he had gone. They would all think he was still asleep.

Michele had never covered the distance between the inn and Angelo's cottage so quickly. He slid and slipped, stumbled and rolled; he jumped from one rock to another. This was the Sunday he had been waiting for, but as he ran he didn't think of the adventure that was only a few hours away. He thought only of what he would say to Angelo.

"Angelo!"

"Michele!"

"Angelo!" Michele dropped down on the sand, too exhausted to talk. "Angelo!"

"That is my name."

"Angelo, listen." Michele gasped for breath. "Angelo, you know how it is with Pietro and me. We are friends—no, we are more than friends, we are brothers. We have different mothers and fathers, but still we are brothers. Inside we are brothers. You know how it is, Angelo."

"Yes, Michele, I know."

"Well, Angelo, last night Pietro came by and—well, you know Pietro and I are always together on Sunday and—oh, Angelo, Angelo, couldn't we take Pietro with us to the cove?"

"Take Pietro!"

"Please, Angelo, please!"

"Pietro? And his donkeys? He will bring his donkeys too, I suppose?"

"Oh, Angelo!"

"Well, how am I to know? First Herre Nordstrom is going to the cove and everyone is frightened to death. Then I, big, brave Angelo, I am going too! Then presto! everyone is going. Lord Derby, Monsieur Jacques, Signor Pagano, Michele! And now Pietro too! Tell me, how am I to know that Pietro's donkeys will not want to go also?"

"But just one more, Angelo, just Pietro?"

"Just one more. Just one more. Why do we waste our time like this? I'll tell you what we should do, Michele. We should put up a sign in the market place. It should read something like this:

" 'ATTENTION!

" 'TODAY AT TWELVE O'CLOCK THERE WILL BE AN EXPEDITION TO THE COVE.

" 'EVERYONE INVITED!

" 'FREE LUNCH. COME AND BRING THE CHILDREN.'

"Then in large red letters we should add:

" 'THIS IS A GREAT SECRET. DO NOT TELL ANYONE.' "

"Oh, Angelo!"

"Well, where will he sit? There are three boats and six people. Two people to a boat."

"Pietro is not very big. He and I together are not as big as Herre Nordstrom. We will make ourselves very small. You will see."

"Well—"

"Oh, Angelo! I knew you would!"

"Did I say yes?"

"You didn't say no."

"All right, we will leave it that way, I didn't say no."

"Then it is all right? I can ask him to go with us?"

"I didn't say no."

"Oh, Angelo, you are wonderful! You always fix everything."

"I have not said no yet, but if you stand there talking and

wasting my time, there is no telling what I might say. Go! Go, before I change my mind."

"Thank you, Angelo. Thank you."

"Go! And be back before noon, so you can help me load the boats."

"Load the boats? What are you putting into them?"

"Not you, unless you hurry. Go! Go! Go!"

Once more Michele started off, clambering over rocks and cobblestones—falling, slipping, sliding—crawling, pulling, grabbing—jumping, running, racing.

Pietro lived on the other side of the island. There was not much time.

Finally he stood in front of Pietro's house. "Pietro! Pietro!"

There was no answer. Michele called. He rattled the door. He knocked and shouted and called again. "Pietro! Pietro!"

Only the donkeys were at home. They stood, huddled together in their little yard, looking the way donkeys always look on Sunday, bewildered by so much leisure.

"Pietro!" Michele couldn't believe that he wasn't at home. He had to be home. On this day of all days he had to be home.

But he wasn't. No amount of shouting or calling would bring him.

Where could he be? Where had he gone? Suddenly the little island of Capri seemed very large—the beach, the roads, the village of Capri, Anacapri, the steps, the mountains. Where should he look for his friend? Where would Pietro go? Why had he gone?

Why? Suddenly Michele knew why he had gone away. Pietro was lonely, disappointed. His best friend had deserted him. He wanted to be by himself.

Michele, standing alone in front of Pietro's cottage, thought he knew how Pietro felt. How would he, Michele, feel if Pietro had done the same thing to him? What would he do? Where would he go?

At that moment Michele knew where Pietro had gone. He had gone to their special place up in the mountains, the place where Michele had taken Lord Derby to paint. They had discovered it, he and Pietro, many years before. Since then it had been their special meeting place, their secret retreat. It was the place they went when they were especially happy, or especially disappointed.

Michele looked up at the sky. Could he get to the top of the mountain and back by noon? What if he were late? Would they go without him? Michele rubbed his hands over his forehead and tried to think. The men might be willing to wait for him, but not the tide. If they hoped to get into the cave and out again during low tide they would have to leave right at noon. With or without Michele, they would have to leave. Standing there, Michele knew that was true. There would be no waiting for anyone today.

Michele looked at the sky again. Could he make it? Should he take the chance? If he started back to the harbor now he would get there in plenty of time. Angelo had asked him to come early and help load the boats. Was it more important to help Angelo or find Pietro? After all, he had tried to find Pietro and he wasn't at home. Certainly, he, Michele, could not be blamed for that. He had done the best he could. Perhaps, by evening, it would not make any difference anyway. Perhaps Pietro would be lucky if he didn't go.

Michele started to run. Even while he was thinking, even while he was looking at the sun, he began to run. He had to find Pietro. Even if he was late, even if he missed going to the cove, he had to find Pietro.

For the third time that morning Michele ran as if possessed. Rocks and stones, dust and dirt, scattered behind him. His clothes were torn, his hands scratched, his feet cut, but Michele scarcely noticed. He passed the village of Capri, the road that led to their inn, the steps to Anacapri. Finally he was on the little hidden path which led to the top of the mountain. He remembered how he had told Lord Derby that it was only a few feet farther to the top. A few feet farther! Michele lunged forward. He parted the bushes and looked around him. "Pietro!"

There was the sky and the sea and the cliffs—but no Pietro.

"Pietro!"

Had he come all this way, probably missed going to the cove, only to find that he had been wrong? Why had he been so sure that Pietro would be here? It had been a wild guess—nothing more.

"Pietro! Pietro!" And the mountains answered back, "Pietro! Pietro!"

"Pietro! Pietro!" Tears came to Michele's eyes. Standing

there on the mountaintop, he felt more lonely and disappointed than he had ever felt before. The cove seemed very far away—too far away. The trip back down the mountainside seemed unbearably long.

"Pietro! Pietro!" And again the mountains echoed. They seemed to be taunting him, teasing him. "Pietro! Pietro!"

Michele knew he should start back. Every second counted, but he felt too exhausted to move. He felt too tired to do anything except stand and call. "Pietro! Pietro!"

He found himself waiting for the echo. But this time his own name came back in answer. "Michele!"

"Michele! Michele!" Pietro's eyes peered around the edge of a cliff. "Michele!"

"Pietro!" Michele gasped, stared at Pietro for a minute as if he could not believe his eyes, then turned and fled down the path. "Pietro, come quickly!" he called back over his shoulder. "There is not a minute to lose. I'll tell you all about it as we go."

It was a strange conversation.

Michele leaped from rock to rock like a young goat. Pietro, confused and puzzled, leaped after him. Sometimes they were close together, sometimes as much as fifty feet apart. Michele shouted, but most of what he said was lost to Pietro.

"I can't hear you," Pietro kept shouting. "I don't know what you're talking about. What are you saying, Michele? What are you saying?"

And all the while strange words drifted back to him: "—Herre Nordstrom—philosophy—the cove—Angelo—

Monsieur Jacques—Lord Derby—Papa—Angelo—three boats—Angelo—the tides—Angelo—noon—Angelo—today —Angelo—*hurry!*"

The "hurry!" was all that Pietro could understand—that and the fact that Michele had not deserted him after all. Whatever Michele was doing, he, Pietro, was doing too. That was all that mattered.

X. THE END—AND THE BEGINNING

When Michele and Pietro reached Angelo's cottage it was deserted.

Had the men gone? Were they too late? Michele looked up at the sky. The sun seemed directly above him. He shaded his eyes and looked out across the water. There was not a boat in sight.

"Pietro, they've gone! They've gone!" Michele's voice cracked and he ended with a sob. Exhausted, he dropped to the ground. His one chance for a real adventure was over. After weeks of hoping and dreaming and planning, he had missed it by a few minutes, perhaps even a few seconds. "They've gone," he repeated dully. "Gone."

"Gone?" Pietro looked at him. "Where have they gone?"

"Where? To the cove, of course."

"*What* cove?"

"What *cove?*"

"Yes."

"Pietro, I told you all about it as we came down the mountain."

Pietro laughed. "You told the wind, Michele, not me. All I heard was a jumble of words, and one strange word I never heard before. Phil—phil—philosophy! Was that it, Michele? What does it mean, this philosophy?"

Michele shrugged his shoulders. "That is what all of us were supposed to find out today."

"What?" Pietro stared at Michele. "We were going out in boats to find the meaning of a word? Who was to tell us—the fish?"

"No, the cove."

"What cove?"

"*The* cove!"

"*The* cove?" Pietro shook his head. This was too much for him. To go to the cove was bad enough, but to go there in order to find the meaning of a word! Pietro looked around him. There were no boats, no sign of anyone anyplace. Angelo's cottage looked as it always looked. He had probably gone fishing—nothing more.

"Michele?"

"Yes, Pietro?"

"Michele, I don't think anyone has gone anyplace. I think this is something you dreamed last night. Too much spaghetti perhaps."

Michele sat up. To miss the trip was bad enough, but to have Pietro think it was nothing but a dream, a nightmare—he couldn't stand that.

"Pietro, listen. One day I heard Herre Nordstrom talking about philosophy. I asked him what it meant, and he tried to tell me. He said all philosophers search for the truth, but I didn't understand what he meant. Then, one night, when Papa told Monsieur Jacques about the cove, Herre Nordstrom got very excited. He said there were many ways to search for the truth, and if we went to the cove and found out the truth about it, he could explain to me what he meant. He—"

Suddenly Michele remembered. He began to run. "Pietro, come. Come! Giovanni and Antonio were to bring their boats to the Grande Marina pier. Perhaps we can catch them there." Michele stopped talking. He needed his breath for running; there was none left over for words.

The pier was only a short distance from Angelo's cottage, but one had to be half fish to get there. That didn't bother Michele. He ran down the beach, plunged into the water, swam quickly around the high rocks jutting into the bay, scrambled onto the beach again, and continued to run. Only once did he look up—and that was a backward glance to see if Pietro was following him. He was, and that was all Michele wanted to know. He ran, his eyes glued to the sand. The beach was covered with rocks and boulders, and he couldn't afford to fall or stumble. There was no time for that.

Finally he allowed himself to look up. There, in front of him, was the Grande Marina and—it was too good to be true —there were the three boats, there were the three guests, there were his father and Angelo. He stumbled now, but it didn't matter. Half running, half falling, he hurried toward them.

"Michele!"

"Where have you been?"

"We were worried about you!"

"We thought you were asleep, but when we looked in your room you weren't there."

Michele stood in front of them, panting. His only answer to all of their questions was a foolish grin. His morning had been filled with a series of wild dashes from one place to another, but now everything was all right. The boats were here. The men were here. He was here, and Pietro—Pietro was here too.

"Well"—Angelo looked around him—"do we start or don't we? Or perhaps we are waiting for Pietro's donkeys?" He picked up a large lunch basket and put it into one of the boats.

Michele stared at the basket. Was it really filled with rocks, as his mother had promised? Suddenly he realized that he had had nothing to eat since Saturday evening. Now it was noon on Sunday. Michele thought of his morning. He had run from the inn to Angelo's cottage; from Angelo's cottage to Pietro's house; from Pietro's house to the top of the mountain; from the top of the mountain to Angelo's cottage; from Angelo's cottage to the Grande Marina. He was sure he had never been so hungry in all his life.

"Papa?"

"Yes, Michele?"

"What's in the basket?"

"I don't know, Michele. Your mother handed it to me

just as we were leaving. I haven't had time to look inside."

"Papa, may I look and see?"

"Look, look! Of course you can look. But you know what your mother said—a basketful of rocks."

Michele lifted the white cloth that covered the basket and peered inside: fresh bread and cheese, smoked fish and olives, grapes and oranges.

"Papa? Look!"

Signor Pagano lifted the white cloth as Michele had done.

"Michele," he said slowly, "I think Mamma understands after all."

Michele tried to swallow the lump in his throat, but the more he swallowed the larger it grew.

"Here." Signor Pagano reached into the basket and broke off a piece of bread and some cheese. "Here, Michele. You are hungry, yes?"

"Yes." Michele took the bread and cheese gratefully. But even after he had eaten, the lump was still in his throat. He knew it would take more than bread and cheese to make it disappear.

"Well!" Angelo waved his hands in the air. "Do I get some help or don't I? Are we going to stay here all day, talking and eating? Soon, perhaps, tea will be served, and someone will arrange a bouquet of flowers. Meanwhile the sun does not stand still, and the tide doesn't either."

Michele jumped out of the boat. "What is it, Angelo? What can I do to help?"

Angelo pointed to a large iron kettle filled with tar. "Here. Put this into the first boat."

Michele stared at the kettle. "Angelo, what do we need with a kettle of tar?"

"To burn."

"To burn?"

"Of course. To burn for light inside the cave."

"But we have torches."

"Torches! A torch in a cave is as reliable as a snowflake in an oven. Listen, Michele. Do not let that lunch basket of your mother's fool you. This is no holiday outing. We are going into a cove where no one that we know has ever been before. Then we are going into a cave that has the ocean for a floor and an opening so small I am not even sure these small boats will be able to get through it. Who knows what winds blow inside that cave? What currents? What drafts? Who knows how strong they will be? Who knows what we will find there? And whatever we find, I want to see it. This kettle of tar—once it is lit only the devil himself will be able to blow it out."

"Only the devil himself!" Michele stared at the kettle. It looked like a witch's caldron, and smelled worse. It was like a symbol of evil. When Angelo lit the tar and the bright flames leaped up, what would they show inside the cave?

A few minutes later the boats were loaded. Silently they took their places. Herre Nordstrom and Angelo were in the first boat; Monsieur Jacques and Lord Derby in the second;

Signor Pagano, Michele, and Pietro in the third. Silently they picked up their oars. Silently they began to row.

The water splashed against the boats. The oars rose and fell and rose again. No one said a word. There was nothing to say. All the talking was over; only the doing remained.

When they were almost at the cove Angelo pulled in his oars and listened. Not a sound came from the cave.

"Ah!" Herre Nordstrom looked pleased. "I hear nothing. Do you hear anything, Angelo?"

"Nothing."

"Well, that is good, eh, Angelo?"

"I don't know."

"You don't know? Why not?"

"It is too quiet."

"Too quiet? Listen to the man! First you tried to frighten us with tales of moaning and groaning, of clanking chains and grating doors. Now you are trying to make us afraid of the silence."

Angelo shook his head. "All silence is not good, Herre Nordstrom, just as all noise is not bad."

"But silence? Who can be afraid of silence? It is nothing."

"There can be a reason for silence, Herre Nordstrom, just as there can be a reason for noise. And if I were going to hide, Herre Nordstrom, I would feel safer behind silence than behind the loudest noise in all the world."

"What are you trying to say, Angelo? What are you afraid of? What do you think is waiting for us in the cave?"

Angelo shrugged his shoulders. "I know no more about

the cave than you do, Herre Nordstorm. I have told you that no one knows about it. I can only say this: the man with the best imagination knows the most, because only he can begin to guess what is inside." Angelo shuddered. The fear of the cove which hovered over everyone on Capri seemed suddenly to envelop him. He could not shake it off.

"That is wonderful, Angelo, what you just said: that the man with the best imagination knows the most about the cave. That is true about everything, Angelo. Men dream, and then they run to catch up with their dreams. That is progress, Angelo. We need both kinds of men—the dreamers and those who try to make the dreams come true."

"And the rowers—we need the rowers too, eh, Herre Nordstrom? We could not go far without the rowers." Angelo smiled, and with his smiling he seemed to shake off his fear of the cove. He picked up his oars and began to row vigorously.

A few minutes later they were inside the cove. The small opening of the cave yawned before them.

"Now, Herre Nordstrom, I am going to light the tar. Then I want you to lie down flat in the boat. The mouth of the cave is so low you will not be able to get through otherwise. I will get out of the boat and push it as I swim. The opening is too narrow to use the oars."

The rest of them waited at the entrance to the cove. They saw Angelo light the tar. They saw Herre Nordstrom lie down in the bottom of the boat. They saw Angelo climb out, grab the boat with one hand, and start to swim. They saw the bright flames of the tar against the black opening.

Then the flames disappeared, the boat disappeared, and finally Angelo too disappeared inside the cave.

Not a sound could be heard. They waited and waited. Still not a sound.

Then, suddenly, there were excited calls and shouts.

"Come! Come quickly!"

"Come! Come quickly!"

The words echoed and re-echoed and echoed again. The calls and the echoes joined, separated, joined together. No one could tell which were the calls and which the echoes.

There was excitement in the words, but still they had a strange, hollow sound. Were they cries for help? Had Angelo and Herre Nordstrom called? Or were the words just a trick to get the other two boats inside the cave?

"Come!"

"Come!"

Monsieur Jacques and Lord Derby picked up their oars and shot ahead. Then Lord Derby lay down in the boat, and Monsieur Jacques, like Angelo, pushed the boat through the small opening.

Again there was silence, and again the excited calls. "Come! Come quickly!"

And again the hollow, echoing sound. "Come! Come quickly!"

Without a word Michele picked up his oars and began to row. Without a word he shipped his oars and dived into the water at the opening of the cave. Without a word Signor

Pagano and Pietro stretched themselves out on the bottom of the boat. Michele started to swim, pushing the boat before him.

Swish!

A great suction seemed to draw them in. One minute they were outside, with all the waters of the bay around them. The next minute they were inside the cave. No, not inside the cave—inside another world.

They all stared.

It was a world made of blue. The light, the water, the rocks, the walls of the cavern, the arched dome—everything was blue. Blue flames of light leaped across the walls. Blue flames rose from the shimmering water. Whether the flames were hot or cold, no one knew, no one cared.

It was too beautiful to believe.

They looked around them. Blue was no longer a color. It was something to touch, to smell, to taste, to hear. Even the air they breathed was blue. And their bodies, filled with it, felt light and buoyant.

Were they bewitched?

Where were they?

What was this place?

It was eerie and strange and gloriously wonderful.

The light, the air, the water, the rocks—all were made of the same material. *Blue!* Blue was the substance of everything; only the shades were different. The air was light blue, the light lighter blue. The water was deep blue, the rocks darker.

Then suddenly the blue was tinged with silver. Every ripple was edged with gleaming bubbles; every wave carried with it a trail of spangles. The boats, the oars, the hands of the men when they dipped them into the water—all were outlined with a spray of diamonds.

It was a world of magic.

No one spoke. They sat as if enchanted. The monsters, the pirates, the man-eating fish had all vanished. In their place was a fairyland that twinkled and gleamed, sparkled and danced, like a flaming sapphire.

They were in the midst of a miracle.

Then Herre Nordstrom began to speak. He spoke softly, as if fearful of disturbing the blue. "Look!" He pointed to some steps at the end of the cavern. "See, those steps go down under the water. Surely they were not always like that. This cavern, this grotto, has all been changed. An earthquake, many years ago, must have caused it to sink. Perhaps that was the beginning of the wild tales about it, I don't know. Perhaps no one will ever know. It is easy to see how these blue flames of light, seen from the outside, would be very frightening." He looked around him. "Most of the monsters men fear are in their minds. They would vanish like smoke if we would only let them. See"—he pointed to the mouth of the cave—"the opening is very small. Almost all the light that enters must pass through the water. Since the water is blue, the light is blue, and everything it touches becomes blue also. It is a gift that nature has made for Capri."

Monsieur Jacques shook his head. "I have traveled all over

the world," he said. "I have seen wonderful things—but nothing I have seen compares with this. The whole world will come to Capri to see it." He smiled at Signor Pagano. "Remember?" he said. "Remember? I said I came to Capri in search of adventure. Never in my wildest dreams did I expect to find an adventure as wonderful as this."

Lord Derby shook his head. "Remember?" he said. "I said I came to Capri in search of beauty. Beauty!" He looked around him. "No one in the world has ever seen anything more beautiful than this."

Herre Nordstrom smiled. "I will tell you," he said, "what all philosophers know. To search for the truth is always an adventure—and there is always beauty in the truth itself. To have knowledge and understanding, to know the truth about things, that can be as exciting and beautiful as this blue cavern, this blue grotto." He looked at Michele and smiled. "Does this help you understand the meaning of philosophy?"

Michele nodded his head, but before he had time to answer Angelo's voice filled the grotto. "Come. We must hurry."

"Hurry? Why?" Everyone started at Angelo. Why should they hurry? The tide would not be high enough to cover the entrance for at least three hours.

"*Stupidos!*" Angelo waved his hands in the air. "Don't you want to tell the people of Capri what we have found? If we hurry they will have time to come here this afternoon." Angelo stopped talking and smiled to himself. "What do you think they will say? How will they act? Hurry. I can't wait to see their faces."

As they rowed back to the Grande Marina pier they made plans. Michele, as soon as they landed, was to run to the inn, tell Signora Pagano what had happened, and bring her to the piazza in front of the church. Angelo was to find the priest and have him ring the church bells. The others were to moor the boats and then go to the piazza.

The village priest was standing in the doorway of the church when Angelo appeared. He saw that Angelo was excited and wondered why he was running, but he was completely unprepared for Angelo's violent outburst.

"The bells!" Angelo shouted to him from the road. "The bells. Ring them!"

"Ring the bells?" The priest stared. "Why? What has happened? An accident? A death? A drowning?"

By this time Angelo had crossed the piazza and was at the foot of the steps. "What is it?" the priest called down to him. "Tell me, Angelo."

"There is no time." Angelo raced up the steps. "Every minute is precious. Ring the bells, I beg you."

The priest did not move. "I cannot ring the bells, Angelo, until I know what has happened."

Now it was Angelo's turn to stare. There was not time to tell his story twice—once to the priest and again to the people. The tide was rising every minute. "Please." Angelo spread his hands in supplication. "Please ring the bells.

When everyone is assembled I will tell you, all together, what has happened."

Still the priest did not move. "The bells are rung for services, for weddings, when someone has died, and for catastrophes," he repeated. "I cannot ring the bells until I know what has happened."

Angelo rushed past the priest and into the church. "*I* know what has happened," he called back over his shoulder, "so *I* can ring them." And before the priest could stop him he entered the bell chamber and began to pull on the ropes.

Never had Capri heard such bell ringing. Each villager, as he rushed from his house, was sure he, his family and the bell ringer were the only living survivors on the island; for surely nothing less than a complete catastrophe would bring forth such a din. Had there been an earthquake? A tidal wave? Had the island been invaded? Everyone hurried to the piazza.

Louder and louder the bells rang. Angelo, pulling hard at the ropes, could not hear the sharp protests of the priest, and since his back was turned toward the doorway, could not see him either.

"Angelo, Angelo," the priest shouted, waving his arms. But the only answer he got was the ringing of the bells, louder and louder.

Not until the piazza was filled with people did Angelo stop. At least he stopped pulling the ropes, but in his own ears the bells continued to ring. He could hear them as he hurried through the church. He could hear them when he stood at the top of the steps and motioned for silence. He could still hear them ringing when he started to talk.

"People of Capri," he said. At least he hoped that was what he said. That was what he meant to say, and those were the words his lips formed, but he himself could hear nothing.

As quickly as possible he told them what had happened. It didn't take long. Then he tried to describe to them the beauty of the cave. That was harder to do. But at last he was finished, and as he stopped speaking the ringing, too, seemed to stop. Now there was silence everywhere.

It was a strange silence. Angelo looked from one face to another questioningly. Where were the shouts of joy? Where were the congratulations? Why didn't the people look pleased, happy, excited? This was a moment for rejoicing. Why was everyone silent?

At last the silence was broken, but not in the way Angelo had expected. The people whispered and murmured to each other. They looked angry and displeased. Then suddenly the murmurings grew louder; the voices more shrill. Still standing at the top of the steps Angelo could hear what they were saying.

"This is some wild dream of Angelo's."

"It is a joke—and a bad one at that."

"It's a trick he's trying to play on us."

"Look, even the priest is angry. He glares at Angelo."

"Angelo has told some big stories in his day, but nothing as bad as this."

"To mention the cove is bad enough—but to say that he went there—"

"How does he dare?"

"And on the church steps, too."

"And before the priest."

"And on Sunday!"

The murmurings grew louder and louder. Then, turning their backs on Angelo, the people began to leave the piazza.

It was then that Signora Pagano, who had been waiting with Michele at the edge of the crowd, hurried forward. She ran up the church steps and, standing beside Angelo, said in a firm voice, "Stop! Wait a minute."

It was surprising how well her voice carried. Everyone heard her, and turned around. They stared at her questioningly. What was she doing there beside Angelo. What did she want to say?

Signora Pagano had never spoken to a crowd of people before, but she didn't think of that as she stood there at the top of the steps. She had heard from Michele the same story Angelo had told, and she knew it was true. The men had gone to the cove and returned safely; that in itself was wonderful. But wonderful, too, had been the look on Michele's face when he told her what they had seen. So much beauty was unbelievable, but if Michele said it was there she was ready to believe it.

But the people didn't believe it. They were turning away from Angelo with angry words. She had heard sharp threats and dangerous mutterings as she hurried through the crowd. Something had to be done—and quickly.

In the same quiet, firm voice Signora Pagano began to speak to the people in the piazza. She told them how Herre Nordstrom had insisted upon going to the cove. She told them how the past month had been filled with plans and work and worry. She told them how the five men and two boys had gone off that morning in three boats, and how they had all returned safe and sound and full of wonder. Then, taking Angelo's hand, she smiled up at him and said, "Come, Angelo, show me your cave."

Once more the people were silent. Signora Pagano, her head held high and her hand on Angelo's arm, walked down the steps, across the piazza and onto the road.

That was the start of a strange procession. First there were Signora Pagano and Angelo, leading the way. Then came the three guests, Signor Pagano, Michele and Pietro, looking very pleased with themselves. And behind them followed the people of Capri, as if bewitched. Down the steep path to the Grande Marina pier they walked. No one spoke. Tension and excitement hung around them.

Arriving at the pier, Angelo and Signor and Signora Pagano got into the first boat. The three guests, Michele and Pietro climbed into the other two. The crowd, waiting on the pier, watched them row fearlessly out toward the mysterious cove.

The cove, however, is some distance from the Grande Marina pier. The waiting crowd would need boats, too, if they were really to see this strange expedition. Instantly every fisherman thought of his own boat tied to the pier, and the scramble that followed was a sight to see. Never on Capri had fishermen's boats been so highly valued; never had fishermen's families felt so superior. In a few minutes the pier was almost empty, and every boat was filled. Still in the same order, the procession had transferred itself to the water.

When the first three boats entered the cove, the other boats formed a wide arc out in the bay. It was as if, with their semicircle of boats, the fishermen were outlining the wide berth they had given the cove for so many years.

It was all like a special performance. The cove was the stage, the first three boats were the scenery, their occupants were the actors, and the people of Capri, seated in their boats, were certainly a most attentive audience.

One by one the three boats disappeared into the cave. The people of Capri, watching and waiting, were still silent.

Seconds took on the length of hours. Would the boats never appear again? Why didn't they come out? What was keeping them inside that cave?

Then slowly the bow of a boat appeared, and a second later the smiling face of Signora Pagano emerged from the bottom of the boat. Like the main actress in a play she nodded and smiled at her audience; and the audience, delighted to see her, shouted and cheered.

Then, as if it had all been pre-arranged, the people in the first three boats on the right of the semicircle started toward the cove. In they went and out again, and as they reappeared their faces showed plainly the wonder they had seen.

Now, at last, the gay mood which Angelo had expected enveloped the crowd. People laughed and talked. Men called from boat to boat. Children shouted and cheered. A song was started, and a hundred voices joined in the chorus. Soon everyone was singing.

Three by three the boats continued to take their turns, and with every trip the hilarity mounted. Never had Capri seen such gay rejoicing.

The last boat got out of the grotto just in time. After that the high tide waters lapped around the top of the entrance, almost hiding it from view. Now the curtains were closed. The performance was over.

But the crowd was still gay. This, they knew, was not the end; it was instead just the beginning.

It was indeed just the beginning. From the east and the west, from the north and the south, by ones and twos, by tens and twenties, by hundreds and thousands, people have come to see this wonder. And each day the tides open wide the entrance, and reveal again one of the most beautiful places in all the world—the famous Blue Grotto on the Island of Capri.